NUMBER TWENTY-SEVEN — 2018

New Millennium WRITINGS

Winner of a Golden Press Card Award for Excellence

Edited by Alexis Williams Carr

This issue has been dedicated to:

Larry Harvey
January 11, 1948—April 28, 2018

ESTABLISHED IN 1996
Special thanks to the Tredup family of Kenosha, WI, Rod Williams of Nashville, TN, and John and Margie Richardson, of Seymour, TN, who were present at the birth.

PUBLISHED ANNUALLY
by New Millennium Writings *with ♥ in Knoxville, Tennessee.*
Email: hello@newmillenniumwritings.org
Phone: 646-798-MUSE

TWICE-ANNUAL NEW MILLENNIUM WRITING AWARDS
For official rules and guidelines of the NMW Writing Awards, and noncontest submissions, please visit our website or see page 190 for details.

ISSN: 1086-7678 ISBN: 978-1-944977-27-6 [PAPERBACK] CPDA BIPAD No. 89927

NEWMILLENNIUMWRITINGS.ORG | SUNSHOTS.ORG | MUSEPAPER.ORG

SUNSHOT PRESS musepaper.org

CONTENTS

New Millennium Writings, Issue 27, 2018

AWARD WINNERS AND FINALISTS

NEW MILLENNIUM WRITINGS

POETRY SUITE 2018

PHOTO ESSAY

WRITING ADVICE FROM THE WINNERS

CONTRIBUTORS

BACK MATTERS

AWARD-WINNERS AND FINALISTS OF

The Twice-Annual

NEW MILLENNIUM WRITING AWARDS

XLIII & XLIV

22

YEARS OF AWARDING & AMPLIFYING POETS AND WRITERS

2,400

NEW & EMERGING WRITERS PUBLISHED TO DATE

$11,000

IN CASH PRIZES AWARDED IN 2018

COUNTRIES ENTERING SUBMISSIONS IN 2018

Australia
Austria
Belgium
Brazil
Canada
China
Costa Rica
Croatia
Cyprus
Czech Republic
Denmark
Finland
France
Germany
Gibraltar
Guernsey
Hong Kong
India
Ireland
Israel
Italy
Jamaica
Japan
Korea
Malta
Netherlands
New Zealand
Norway
Philippines
Poland
Portugal
Romania
Saudi Arabia
Singapore
South Africa
Spain
Sri Lanka
Sweden
Switzerland
Taiwan
U.A.E.
United Kingdom
U.S.A.

First-time-awarded and _first-time-published-in-print_ distinctions remain in the majority here, making up 62% of the last four writing contests.

The editors and judges at

NEW MILLENNIUM WRITINGS

are pleased to announce the

44TH NEW MILLENNIUM POETRY AWARD

MARY MAKOFSKE

of Warwick, New York

"DOLDRUMS NEAR THE END OF EMPIRE"

POETRY FINALISTS | AWARDS XLIV

Sarah Van Arsdale, New York, New York..."Undertow"

Rachel Berghash, New York, New York..."Dialogue and Chorus"

Anna Bernsein, Brooklyn, New York ..."Fly Trap"

Harlan Bjornsad, Valparaiso, Indiana..."Perennial Selection"

Bill Garten, Hudson, Ohio..."Packing"

Megan Gieske, Newton, New Jersey..."The Makura-kazari"

Georganne Harmon, Nashville, Tennessee..."And Clay"

Desiree Hellegers, Portland, Oregon..."Kodak Moments"

Ryan Hibbett, Sycamore, Illinois..."Having Booked a Vasectomy"

Trish Lindsey Jaggers, Smiths Grove, Kentucky..."The Dinghy Speaks of Sinking"

Nicole Johnson, Del Mar, California..."First Prayer"

Jen Karetnick, Miami Shores, Florida..."Elegy for a Gambler"

Katharyn Machan, Ithaca, New York..."Gingerbread"

Berwyn Moore, Erie, Pennsylvania..."Fig Tree"

Lisa St John, Cottekill, New York..."The Whens of Now"

Ken Stahl, Tucson, Arizona..."For Judi"

Shay Alexi, Atlanta, Georgia..."RIPE or PRO-LIFE or THE DEFINITION OF LIVING"

Ruth Thompson, Hilo, Hawaii ..."Hero's Return"

Vernon Waring, King of Prussia, Pennsylvania..."Conclusion"

Laura Budofsky Wisniewski, Hinesburg, Vermont..."In Favor of Emotional Eating"

The editors and judges at

NEW MILLENNIUM WRITINGS

are pleased to announce the

43RD NEW MILLENNIUM POETRY AWARD

KATIE BICKHAM

of Shreveport, Louisiana

"SHORN"

POETRY FINALISTS | AWARDS XLIII

Sarah Van Arsdale, New York, New York..."Taken"

Akesha Baron, Seattle, WA..."Home Is about the Light"

Nan Becker, New Jersey..."Verity"

Carolyn Evans Campbell, Evergreen, CO..."Red Sequined Shoes at the Top of the World"

Lisa Dordal, Nashville, TN..."Elevator Ride with Famous Poet"

Ryan Lawrence, Portland, OR..."Most Memorable Insult"

Bianca Lech, Steuben, ME..."Desk Poem"

Jerico Lenk, Tampa, FL..."Hylophobia"

Sandy Longley, Delmar, NY..."Nocturne, in Red and Black"

Derek Mong, Crawfordsville, IN..."Exhausted, Renegade Elephant"

Jacob Paul Patchen, Cambridge, OH..."Dog Barking at 4 a.m. on a Wednesday Morning"

Laura Rand, Auburn, CA ..."When a Gibbous Moon Must Do"

Roberta Senechal de la Roche, Charlottesville, VA..."Timepiece"

Cynthia Snow, Shelburne Falls, MA..."Ruby-Topaz Hummingbird with Pinktoe Tarantula"

James R. Stack, Andover, VT..."Applesauce"

Kristen Steenbeeke, Iowa City, Iowa..."Apocalypse Dream Again"

Cathleen Stewart, Rock Hill, SC..."Not One Sparrow"

Jim Glenn Thatcher, Yarmouth, ME..."Spoor"

Sarah Wetzel, New York, NY..."Medea in Middle Age"

James K. Zimmerman, Pleasantville, NY..."Painted Ladies"

The editors and judges at

NEW MILLENNIUM WRITINGS

are pleased to announce the

44TH NEW MILLENNIUM FLASH FICTION AWARD

ADAM SIFRE

of Wayne, New Jersey

"PAPA'S PARROT"

FLASH FICTION FINALISTS | AWARDS XLIV

Alex Apuzzo, Clintondale, NY..."Rain"

Sarah Bradley, East Haven, CT..."Sweet Potato Baby"

Laine Cunningham, Hillsborough, NC..."The Merboy in Her Life"

Madie Dhaliwal, Beverly Hills, California..."Woolmates"

Elizabeth Erbeznik, Austin, TX..."Fly Season"

Jaclyn Fowler, United Arab Emirates..."Mama Joanne"

Joel Freiburger, Glen Ellyn, IL..."A Letter, Three Bodies, and a Car Wreck"

Lorien House, Tijeras, NM..."The Perfect Essay"

Michelle Hsu, Studio City, CA..."Venus, from the Sea"

Eubert McLeod, Bronx, NY..."Fog"

Joe Milan Jr., Las Vegas, NV..."Oarsmen Wanted"

Jason Miller, Bloomington, IN..."What Are the Chances"

Eli Mitchell, Knoxville, TN..."Ferrying the Dread"

Frank Ortega, Cold Spring, NY..."Cherokee Blue"

Sebasian Sangervasi, San Francisco, CA..."Caught"

Susan Segal, Irvine, CA..."Nosalgia"

Jesse Sensibar, Flagstaf, AZ..."One More Reason Not to Sleep with People You Don't Know Very Well"

Luke Tennis, Baltimore, MD..."On Puraran Beach"

Lyzette Wanzer, San Francisco, CA..."Portrait"

Emma Whitehall, Northumberland, United Kingdom..."Litter"

The editors and judges at

NEW MILLENNIUM WRITINGS

are pleased to announce the

43RD NEW MILLENNIUM FLASH FICTION AWARD

MIAH JEFFRA

of San Francisco, California

"GROWL"

FLASH FICTION FINALISTS | AWARDS XLIII

Jocelyn Ajami, Chicago, Illinois... "Reaching the Border"

Andi Dobek, Waterloo, Illinois... "Death by UPS"

Mary Bess Dunn, Nashville, Tennessee... "Closet Tales"

Ekta Garg, Savoy, Illinois... "She's Coming Home"

Amina Gautier, Chicago, Illinois... "Clytaemnaestra "

Claire Guyton, Lewiston, Maine... "God Save Our Queen"

William Hemmig, Stockton, New Jersey... "Brake Pads"

Conor Houghton, Bath, United Kingdom... "The Unfortunate"

Sharon McNeill, Peoa, Utah... "Ashes"

Patricia Poteat, Asheville, North Carolina... "The Girl Who Fell to Heaven"

Lee Reilly, Chicago, Illinois... "Pastor Bob's Picnic"

Mil Norman-Risch, Richmond, Virginia... "Predator"

Leah Silverman, Gladwyne, Pennsylvania... "I smudged the sun today."

Kate Simonian, Lubbock, Texas... "Late Chrysalis, Early Summer"

J Spru, Winterport, Maine... "Hannah"

Sandi Sonnenfeld, Poughkeepsie, New York... "The Insomniac's Book of Lists"

Frank Tavares, Coconut Creek, Florida... "Head in the Hole"

Liza Nash Taylor, Keswick, Virginia... "Scrapbook"

Sabrina Vienneau, Salt Lake City, Utah... "Joy to the World"

Cady Vishniac, Columbus, Ohio... "Panhandle, Gulf"

The editors and judges at

NEW MILLENNIUM WRITINGS

are pleased to announce the

44TH NEW MILLENNIUM FICTION AWARD

EVAN MCMURRY

of Brooklyn, New York

"NOTHING KINKY"

FICTION FINALISTS | AWARDS XLIV

Nancy Allen, Dallas, Texas..."The Gospel of New Eyes"

Alex Apuzzo, Clintondale, New York..."When the Sun Rises"

Raymond Philip Asaph, Long Island, New York..."Working with Sunshine"

Angela Blair, Encino, California..."Safe House"

Chad V. Broughman, Harbor Springs, Michigan..."Check Mate"

Silas Coghill, Roseville, Minnesota..."In the Velocity of Thought"

Mikaila Daniel, Sunrise, Florida..."She Comes with the Rain"

Daniel Draper, Derbyshire, United Kingdom..."The Gardener's Wife"

Paula Friedman, Gresham, Oregon..."The Workings of the Flashlight in the Darkness"

Amalia Gladhart, Eugene, Oregon..."Star Turn"

Gail Israel, Los Angeles, California..."Into The Night Woods"

Deb Jannerson, New Orleans, Louisiana ..."Empty Eyes"

Alexander Jones, Jersey City, New Jersey..."Good Times"

Dennis Littrell, Kula, Hawaii..."Jug Chablis"

Susan Lowell, Tucson, Arizona..."Ironwork"

Tyler Lynch, Somerville, Massachusetts ..."Word for Word"

Michele Ruby, Louisville, Kentucky..."A Little Night Music"

Terri Scullen, Alexandria, Virginia..."Go Fish"

Jusin Vibbert, Sunnyside, New York..."Form and Void"

Bonnie West, Saint Paul, Minnesota..."I'm Here"

The editors and judges at

NEW MILLENNIUM WRITINGS

are pleased to announce the

43RD NEW MILLENNIUM FICTION AWARD

CASSADY BLACK

of Denver, Colorado

"MAPPING HANNA"

FICTION FINALISTS | AWARDS XLIII

Matthew Basiliere, Natick, MA..."Mugging, Parts One Through Three—Hell's Kitchen, 1993"

Lisa Bass, Santa Barbara, CA..."Episode 780: Fruit"

Scott Beggs, Monterey, CA..."Ghost with a Machine"

David Borofka, Clovis, CA..."Flight"

Teresa Burns Gunther, Oakland, CA..."Patch of Grass"

Richard Buxton, United Kingdom..."Little Brothers"

Emily Capdeville, New Orleans, LA..."An Act of Consolation"

Margaret Fox, Toronto, Canada..."Solitary Soul"

Seth Gannon, Portland, OR..."Parking Lots"

Chris Helvey, Patrick Martin, Ireland..."Ideas Machine, Suffolk Street"

Kristina Newberry, Bland, VA..."Nepenthe"

Martha Payne, Atlanta, GA..."Trash"

Susan Redden, Athelstone, South Australia..."The Lottery"

Cathy Rose, San Francisco, CA..."Avatar Trevillian"

Derek Rose, Mechanicville, NY..."Resurface"

Anneliese Schultz, Richmond, Canada..."The Fury and the Words"

J Spru, Winterport, ME..."Decker"

Julianna Waters, Portland, OR..."Bethel Lindy"

Paula Zaby, Sacramento, CA..."As the Twig is Bent"

The editors and judges at

NEW MILLENNIUM WRITINGS

are pleased to announce the

44TH NEW MILLENNIUM NONICTION AWARD

ANNE GUDGER

of Portland, Oregon

"DENDRITES"

NONFICTION FINALISTS | AWARDS XLIV

David Berner, Clarendon Hills, Illinois..."The Runaway"

Laura Carey, Chico, California..."Father Figure"

Ioanna Carlsen, Tesuque, New Mexico..."My Mother Comes from Another World"

Linda Chase, Rhinebeck, New York..."He Was Henry Hudson"

Maryah Converse, Newark, New Jersey..."What Never Happened with Ahmed"

June Mears Driedger, Lansing, Michigan ..."Bearing Witness"

Eden Elief, Dallas, Texas..."The Will To Find a Testament"

Maya Fanjul-Debnam, Minneapolis, Minnesota..."Lessons from my mother"

Megan Fulwiler, Vergennes, Vermont..."Sanctuary Sites"

Calvin Hennick, Milton, Massachusetts..."The World's Most Boring Drinking Problem"

Gina Iaquinta, Brooklyn, New York..."Tastes They Left"

Ella Jacobson, Brooklyn, New York..."Ten Years of Signs"

Lisa Lebduska, Salem, Connecticut..."The Things We Saved"

Sandra Miller, Arlington, Massachusetts..."A Heart Song in Four Chambers"

Varley O'Connor, Cleveland Heights, Ohio..."The Little Coat"

Reg Saner, Boulder, Colorado..."The Road's Motion"

Colette Sartor, Los Angeles, California..."The House on Bentley Avenue"

Morgan Smith, Santa Fe, New Mexico..."Hidden Treasures"

Tomi Tunrarebi, Los Angeles, California..."Orphan"

Mary Wysong-Haeri, Vancouver, Washington..."Black Friday"

The editors and judges at

NEW MILLENNIUM WRITINGS

are pleased to announce the

43RD NEW MILLENNIUM NONICTION AWARD

MICHELE LEAVITT

of Gainesville, Florida

"HIDDEN IN A SUITCASE"

NONFICTION FINALISTS | AWARDS XLIII

Katie Bain, Los Angeles, CA..."Four Days in New Orleans"

M R Branwen, Los Angeles, CA..."Even if I Am Saturn"

Valerie Gardner, Cornville, Arizona..."Fear No Evil"

Charlie Hanline, Pueblo, Colorado..."Five Year Plans and First Kisses"

Nia Ita, Rego Park, New York..."The Night"

Nancy Jainchill, Woodstock, New York..."The Feminist Sex Queen"

Mal King, Santa Paula, CA..."Living Life in Capital Letters"

Jerry Lawrence, Santa Cruz, CA..."Me and Aldo"

Adva Lipson, Derby, Connecticut..."The Secret Life of a School Photographer"

Tan Liu, Redondo Beach, CA..."A-Cruel Accounting"

Olivia Moreton, Salt Lake City, Utah..."Reunion"

Amy Pechukas, Brooklyn, New York..."Fiona"

Dede Ranahan, Lincoln, CA..."Sooner Than Tomorrow"

Elizabeth Rose, Galisteo, New Mexico..."Wearing a Hat from Hell by the Perfect Servant"

Nan Sanders Pokerwinski, Newaygo, Michigan..."Tabu"

Benjamin Shalva, Reston, Virginia..."Head in the Clouds: Navigating...the Digital Age"

Kathleen Tarr, Anchorage, Alaska..."Intimate Translations"

Linda White, Silver Lake, Ohio..."Searching for Home"

Nancy Williams, Weston, Connecticut..."Shoes at Hardee's Hamburgers"

GYV, Minneapolis, Minnesota..."Is this What You Want"

Siang, Ithaca, New York..."We said it with flowers"

New Millennium WRITINGS

You are not going to create community unless
you struggle together with other people.

You will not create community unless
you face survival with other people.

Community isn't about sentiment. It's not
about Kumbaya. It's not about loving other
people, per se. It's about struggling with them,
because only when you struggle together
for survival with other people do you begin
to see their soul. That's how it's done.

—Larry Harvey

1948—2018

ARTIST, ACTIVIST, CO-FOUNDER OF BURNING MAN

Mary Makofske

DOLDRUMS NEAR THE END OF EMPIRE

Better, perhaps, to sit in this autumn sunlight,
warm as summer thanks to our cozy blanket of carbon,

than read another analysis of debates that simmer
with heat, not light, as the campaigns sputter and cough

while we stand hopeless on the sidelines,
knowing no candidate can take us to the land

we remember, with what may be tarnished memory,
or to the one we've never quite reached, far off in the fog.

Under the drowsy confusion of wasps, the flutter
of robins and bluebirds with no yen for the South,

easy to let the eyelids close and enter the blinkered
nirvana of *now*, glad that winter is not already

inserting needles into our flesh. Grateful that bombs
are not today exploding in our markets. And yet—

the thought insinuates itself that whether we keep
God in the Pledge of Allegiance or take God out,

the world grinds on as it always has.
No one has found the antidote to history.

Our nation, glorious in concept, at its most powerful,
most fragile, too will pass, not altogether, but unravel,

as already it has begun to fray, and how will we face
the end of its glory days? Can we settle, bemused

continued

but philosophical, into our status as has-been, backwater?
No, rather bluster and throw ourselves on our swords,

or, more likely, turn our swords on those we blame.
Those lapping the small and shrinking pools of power

will bare their teeth at shadows slinking closer.
Nostalgia will become the drug of choice.

The problem is we can't agree what past to long for.
Our finest moments a bullet lodged in the head of a foe,

or a piece of bread shared with a stranger. Perhaps
a moment of conscience when we acknowledged

how we had failed. My garden staggers on, squash
swelling, draining the life from spent leaves, and kale

impatient for frosty nights. The bees we fear
are vanishing hover over the last ragged flowers,

and the praying mantis my grandson saved in the greenhouse
stalks slowly through its final days. Everything I value

refuses to rush, refuses to be bought or sold, wants
to grow to its peak, then decay. *I won't eat*

what I couldn't kill, says my daughter-in-law,
and maybe we shouldn't kill what we can't eat.

But the day is too beautiful for such thoughts.
I spill out my treasures gathered along the shore,

rinse my hands in stones and beach glass.
What do they mean? Why have I saved them?

They were cliffs, walls, boulders, bottles
that once held sweetness and spirits. Broken,

worn down, polished, they gleamed in water.
How dull they seem in this dry autumn light.

Writing Advice, NMW 2018

Reading breeds writing.

So many "mentors" I've never met have inspired me and shown me how poetry can be done. The longer I write, the more easily poems come, so practice certainly improves the process. But always it's best not to settle for the almost-right. As Mark Doty has said:

"Every poem is a new puzzle, and a big part of being a poet is learning to take pleasure in working it out, learning to tolerate frustration. Every once in a while, a good line or a strong phrase just seems to pop out, but the truth is that most poems are written badly before they're written well. You have to be willing to mess up, say something in a clichéd way, be sentimental or sound dumb. Then you take what you've written and go to work on it. Then stand back, take a break, and go back and work some more."

"Doldrums Near the End of Empire" sat in my "finished" file for a time. But the ending didn't seem to work hard enough, so I kept mulling it over and trying this and that until I felt it had sufficient weight to close the poem.

Mary Makofske

New Millennium
Award for Poetry

"Doldrums Near the End of Empire"

Mary Makofske's latest books are *World Enough, and Time* (Kelsay, 2017) and *Traction* (Ashland, 2011), winner of the Richard Snyder Prize. Her poems have appeared in *Poetry, Southern Poetry Review, Poetry East, Antiphon, Poetry Daily*, and in eighteen anthologies. She received the 2017 International Poetry Prize from *Atlanta Review*.

marymakofske.com

Katie Bickham

SHORN

The Pentecostal woman next door confides:
the Lord forbids a blade touch her hair. It rats
and scrapes her knees, unbeautiful, decades old.
She weeps in the mornings, rakes and breaks
comb teeth through it. Her neck is off. She whispers,
"The nice gay man downtown says he will take me
out back, douse it with perm solution, and clap it off
between two boards." The Lord, she knows,
is merciful.

Not even God can bear our nakedness
and in his kindness, curtained us with hair.
Mine is beautiful. I have seen men's fingers,
possessed, clicking and itching to reach for it,
to catch it in a breeze. It is long, golden,
and as God wills it, when I am unclothed,
it covers almost everything that makes me
woman.

With it, imagine all the saviors' feet
I could anoint with precious oil, on my knees
repentant, weeping. Or put in my place,
towered, chaste, think of all the princes
who could grip it like rope in their sweating fists,
scale my prison, unlock me, liberate me
from witches.

Before crowds, inquisitors shaved witches
bare to seek out the devil's mark. If unmarked,
they tried to coax it out, poured boiling lard
into the women's eyes, navels, vaginas. The devil
marks us all.

Unshorn, we are death itself: serpentine
and secret. Our hair conceals our power
to bear souls into the world, to feed them
from our own flesh: sower, tender, reaper,
shepherd, wolf, wool and fur. For our crimes

in Eden, temples, beds and caves and back
seats, we have been covered by the gods
in hair, snaked by goddesses, marked by devils,
beheaded by heroes and weaponized,
and still your fingers. Your fingers twitch.
You must know what it feels like in your hands.

Perhaps if we let it loose, pin it up, braid it
in one braid, two braids, corn row it,
perhaps if we perm it, straighten it, relax
it, iron it, perhaps if we pick it into an afro,
Perhaps if we shave it, wig it, veil it,
perhaps if we cover it in a habit, so that from the sky,
we are indiscernible from each other,

we will be safe.

Perhaps if we pluck it, wax it into triangles
and thin lines, send electrical signals into the follicles,
Perhaps if we trade it for food, for money,
for train fare, Christmas presents, perhaps if we
let you snip a lock to worship, perhaps if we
let you wrap it around our necks like nooses

we will be safe.

The Russian army found fourteen thousand pounds
of human hair when they took Auschwitz. Bailed
and loose, still curled, ribboned. The hair yet unused
for socks, for mattresses upon which men would dream
of women, for thread, for rope.

Writing Advice, NMW 2018

My creative writing students are always so disappointed when they ask for help with their writing and I just give them a reading list.

My reading to writing ratio is about 20:1, which I think is a healthy ratio for any writer no matter how green or seasoned. I never feel more like writing than when I've read something beautiful and feel white-hot jealousy that some other writer got to it before I did.

I don't write every day or even every week. Sometimes I carve out time to travel somewhere for a few weeks to write nonstop so I can return to my life as a parent and a teacher without trying to divide that with writing. Or, just go with one of my mentors' writing advice: "Find a cheap therapist and pick a liquor."

–Katie Bickham

New Millennium

Award for Poetry

"Shorn"

Katie Bickham's book, *The Belle Mar* (2015), won the Lena-Miles Wever Todd Poetry Prize. Katie's poems have appeared in *Rattle, Southern Quarterly, Prairie Schooner, Pleiades, The Missouri Review,* and elsewhere. She received The Missouri Review Editor's Prize and an SLS fellowship.

Katie teaches creative writing at Bossier Parish Community College.

PAPA'S PARROT

Adam Sifre

HE WASN'T THERE FOR THE BEGINNING or the end. In the beginning, he was still a wild thing. Nothing more than a voice in the chorus of the Dark Continent, back when it was a thing of terrible beauty and attracted people like the old man; people who breathed adventure the way mortals breathe air. In the beginning, he was still part of the place that would twice try to kill the old man, and fail both times.

By then, however, the African Grey had become a Cuban national, and had forgotten all about the jungle. On the small island, its beak and feathers were tempered with rivers of dark rum, fired by a thousand tropical sunsets, and stained with cheap smoke and Royal Deluxe ink.

All these gifts the old man gave the bird. All these and one more. The words. The old man's words. Spoken most often in the small hours, after the bottle was finally shelved and before daybreak would come and ruin everything. The old man spoke, sometimes sober, often not. Concise. Perfect. Slurred. It did not matter. The bird drank them all in equally, soaking them up over ten thousand nights.

The old man spoke through nights that were never exactly quiet. His words were often accompanied by faint strains of the richest music known to man, played in a local bar known to only a few.

After the first year, the bird's cage was always open. During the day it had free reign of the small home. There was a window, and that was always open as well. The bird never left. By then the old man's words had tethered the bird as if they were steel links of chain. At night, though, the bird always returned to his cage, where it waited for the old man to speak.

Sometimes the words were spoken in code, clacked out on a typewriter which was old even then, when such things were often new. The *click-clack* code reminded the parrot of rain, and sometimes this would lull it to sleep and into bird dreams of ghost jungles; places long forgotten in the bird's waking hours.

He was not there for the beginning. But he was there for much. *The Old Man and The Sea* feathered the cage. The words spoken aloud, repeated in *click-clack*, edited, repeated again. The bird remembered. Not all of it, not everything. But enough. The old man–and he *was* old, even to parrots who are in the habit of outliving us all–had a way of writing words that stuck. He had no use for the others.

It was only a matter of time and words, before Papa's parrot began to change. How could it not? If it had been a dog or a cat, or anything else, things might have been different.

A dog is a dog. A cat is a cat. But a parrot? A parrot is always something more than a parrot.

Papa's parrot listened to the Old Man and the Sea. It learned of the fish that was not a fish and was all fish. It bore witness as the old man conjured up the perfect, eternal struggle. The fisherman's simple heartbreak settled on the bird's small, delicate bones, like a piece of fantastical scrimshaw.

Later, much closer to the end, the parrot learned *For Whom the Bell Tolls*, first delivered in a rainstorm of *click-clacks*, and later by Papa's own deep, sawdust voice. The old man spoke and the parrot's eyes would pin in and out in excitement. The words stuck, as they always did, and the parrot remembered and changed again.

One day Papa left. He did not come back. Ketchum, Idaho, is not the sort of ending the Old Man would have chosen to write. It does not stick the way Cuba sticks. But terrible endings were a genetic defect in Papa's family and he could not be faulted for this one.

The parrot knew nothing of Ketchum, Idaho or bad endings. It only knew Papa had left. He had left before. He had always come back. Always he came back to speak to his bird. Always, but not now.

One day a brown man came and took the bird. The brown man kept the bird's cage door closed, but he was a nice man. The bird did not talk any more, but the brown man did not seem to mind. He gave the bird crackers and nuts and water. He cleaned the bird's cage and he talked to the bird in ordinary words that did not stick. The bird enjoyed the crackers and nuts, but it felt alone.

The new room had a small table, but no typewriter. There were no bottles of rum, either full or empty. The brown man did not smoke and there were no stacks of paper. There was no rain patter of words. Not even the faintest strains of the richest music ever known were part of the bird's world anymore. There was only a radio that sometimes played music already robbed of life. The bird's eyes did not pin.

A long time passed.

One night the brown man sat at his desk, listening to something that was not music on the small radio. The bird, Papa's bird, pulled a loose tail feather free with its sharp beak. The feather was sunset red and orange. The bird held it in one claw. The brown man looked at the bird with curiosity. The bird did not drop the feather. Not this one.

"Eighty-four days now without taking a fish."

The words startled the brown man, but only because he had never heard the bird speak. He did not understand what they meant. He was a nice man, but somehow the words did not stick to him.

The claw held the feather turned quill, and for a while the bird made strange motions in the air. Then the bird hopped a little to its right and waited.

The man stared and the bird imagined that the brown man's own eyes were pinning.

"Ink."

The word came out small, almost forlorn. It was the last word Papa's bird ever said. Years later, when the brown man had become an old man himself, but not *the* old man, he would sometimes wonder about that night and the bird's last spoken word. At such times, the old, brown man almost convinced himself that the word had come out as a request.

But it was a fleeting thought, and it did not stick.

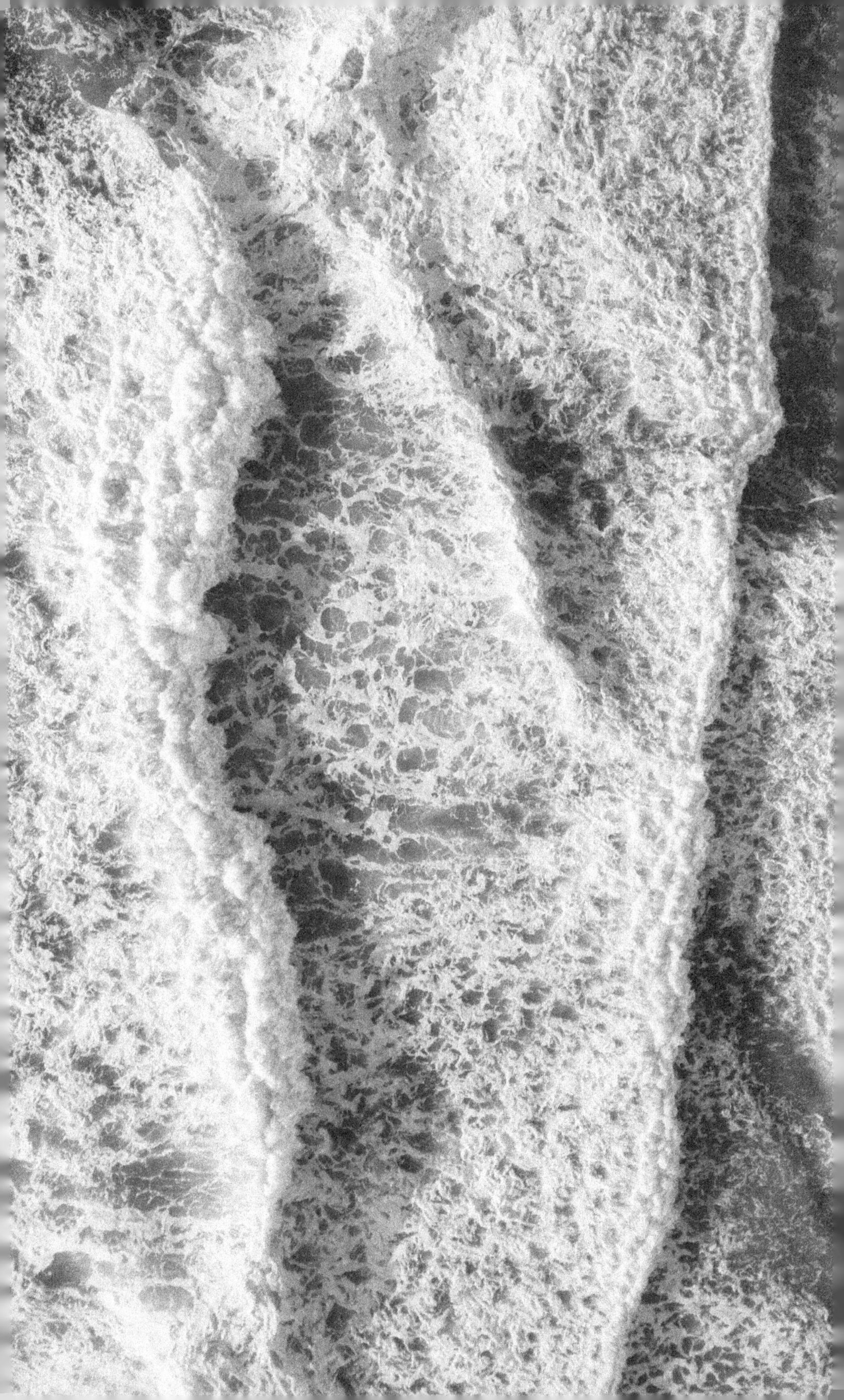

Writing Advice, NMW 2018

I've written a lot of fiction that no one will ever read, so it's important that you pay close attention here. Write as often as possible, and when you're not writing, read.

For short fiction, just sit down and write. For longer stuff, outline. If that doesn't work, try something else. Wake up. Sit down. Write 1,000 words. It's the best advice I have, and it's exactly what I plan on doing someday.

The best stories I've ever read all have one thing in common. The author finished them. Starting things is fun! Like dating. Who doesn't like those first three dates? Especially date number 3! That's the best! Starting a story is like that. But by page 8, it's time to meet his parents, or you're forcing yourself to binge watch *Dr. Who*. You get the idea. A real relationship takes work. It can be a grind. There will be days when you will ask yourself if the whole thing is worth it. There will be times when you're just going through the motions. Days when you're in your car in the driveway, dreading having to go inside.

You're a writer. You know what I'm talking about!

Keep writing!

Adam Sifre

New Millennium
Award for Flash Fiction

"Papa's Parrot"

Adam Sifre is a fifty-something writer, hiding out in the wilds of North Jersey. He has three children, an imaginary dog, and many friends, and suspects none of them have read his work.

He's the author of *I've Been Deader*, a near-perfect blend of horror and comedy.

GROWL

Miah Jeffra

THE RUMBLE COMES FROM DEEP IN THE throat, a low place, breath slow and soaked in the shaping of sound, a snarled pranayama, the chords fold and judder, their own capricious Ring of Fire. We never expect it. Our lips pull up in the way that we signal disgust, or mimic singing a Mötley Crüe song, our nostrils spread open in the scrunch, and the teeth, the canines, specifically, reveal themselves in the snarl. And the sound of gravel, of rumble, of some force coming. *Growl.* We can't even say the word without yielding effort, a full commitment of the mouth to convey the idea. A full, open-wide presence. We are predators, this sound speaks. But what does that mean?

My first memory of it is what one would expect: a dog. A hound. A long slate-gray snout that juts from sagged eyes. A military housing playground in Norfolk, Virginia. I am six. I stand in front of the dog, this creature that appears so snug in the hub of civility, yet a beast. An animal. What makes this one different from the wolf or the bear? My six-year-old genius suspects once peering into the dog, the mystery of this animal soon to be discovered. I stare, committed to the science, my elliptical reflection in the black glass of its droopy eyes. And then it comes, the slow rising rumble, the quivering of slack lip, the teeth, and before I reason enough with my instincts to retreat, the whole mouth upon me, a soft bite, more of a warning than an attack. But the impression holds vivid, not so much the bite but the sound. *Don't fuck with me*, this growl says.

My mother's growl is wild and screeching and involves a frying pan in our trailer park kitchen. Her, in a bathrobe. Her second husband, my stepfather, in his threadbare underwear. The smell of eggs overcooking, garlic and farts. He swarms her with accusations that don't possess much specificity, that grow more abstract with their frequency. "Where were you" and "You should" and "Answer me." My mother's auburn hair crackles dry and electric, knotted on her head, some grabbing down her back and shoulders, autumn straw sprung sideways, reaching out. Bill's litany grows more confident with my mother's silence, more cracking, more adolescent. "You, you, me, you, me, you, you, bitch, you, bitch, me, me, me," and then it emerges: the low rumble, grumble in the throat, the lips, the teeth, and then further, something even more, the rise into a shriek, high in the head and splayed out in three-dimensional space, a noxious sound. And the frying pan, from stove to my stepfather's shoulder, his mouth a big stupid O, my mother's mouth a rack of violence, eggs arcing through the air, steam on its rise off the fury and the food. *Don't fuck with me*, this growl says.

The growl of our stomachs. We hear it, and we think it tells us we hunger. In fact, that is not the case. Our stomachs, our intestines, ceaselessly serve to push, to send things from our mouths to our assholes. It is a loyal and perpetual labor. Smooth muscle contracts in waves, steers the stuff, perhaps fried eggs, through 25 feet of coil. It is always happening, every moment, but we only hear it when our guts are empty. That is when the sound reverberates from inside, suddenly played in an amphitheater for its effort. It is then that we understand the want of the thing. It is an echo of need.

I am fucking a boy in Los Angeles, California. We are in the back seat of my car in the parking structure of Amoeba Records. I meet him in the used CD aisles, between Depeche Mode and Earth, Wind and Fire. It was in the middle of one of many slutty Hollywood interludes. A bell of sweat drops from my nose onto his barely-there chest, smooth muscle, his tiny brown nipples, and then he makes the sound. The growl, teeth and all, eyes fixed. He is telling me, no warning me: *I am an animal. You are a beast. We are all and only nature in this cramped capsule of pleather and plastic and metal and glass.* It works. I get harder than I already am, yet am so hesitant of the hunger—so not as present, in my ambivalence—that I can only giggle, watching my body disappear and reappear into his own, this fleeting boy. *Fuck me*, this growl says.

Growls suppose an incivility. It is up there with ass-picking, pussy-scratching, and hocking snot. We never expect it from ourselves. We *tsk tsk*, we denounce, we condemn its bestial origin, and yet our pupils come alive, alight in our moment, our bodies sweat, get wet, get hard, get sprung. What else does it remind us of? Are we not most beast when most immediate? Don't we always move from mouth to asshole? And isn't it us being our most civil selves, to give warning to our violence, before the bite, before the strike, before the demand to love?

There are people growling everywhere. At any given moment, there must be thousands of growls. A child in Yucaipa howls at her brother—that's my fruit-roll-up. My precious. A tow-truck driver in Oakland knows the roommate is gone, and the roommate's girlfriend has made it very clear that the coast is too with a condom in her teeth, a snarl of its own kind. Every day, there must be nurses, husbands, schoolchildren, baristas, carpenters, parking meter attendants, dog walkers, born-again Christians, vapor clerks that find their paws and claws, their rumble, in the folds of civility. Fathers alone must account for so many growls, the muddle of safeguard and violence so braided in their boyhood. And then there is Angela Cavallo, who lifts a 1964 Chevy Impala to save her teenage son, pinned underneath its metal and glass. Imagine that growl, that echo of need so strong it rattles in the chamber of every heart.

Every time a promise is taken, a promise needs shielding, a promise is about to be fulfilled. An about to, an about to. It's all in the about to happen that we erupt, these growls, these warnings of our immense power; how often, open-wide, we echo in need.

HUMAN
DESIRE
TO BE
HUMAN
DREAM
NEED

Writing Advice, NMW 2018

Writing is a studio practice. And, much like any studio practice, there is no single way to establish that practice. There has been a lot written on the how-to. Some say write every day, for one hour. Some say schedule your writing time, like any other occupation.

I say listen to these suggestions, but do not be dismayed if they don't work for you. There is no single way of writing. Experiment with all kinds of habits, until you find the one that suits your sensibility.

For me? I need to have a whole day with nothing planned, usually, even if I write for only two hours. That typically affords me one good writing day per week. I'd like more, but we have to make a living, absorb experience, and give love to our friends and family. All of it is necessary, since writing is a total practice, informed by the observed tensions of our lives.

Oh, and embrace revision. In fact, think of revision as writing something new every time. Re-vision. See again. And again. Because it is something new, every time.

Miah Jeffra

NEW MILLENNIUM
AWARD FOR FLASH FICTION

"Growl"

Miah Jeffra is the author of *The First Church of What's Happening* (Nomadic Press, 2017). They have been awarded the Sidney Lanier Prize and Clark-Gross Award for fiction, and a 2014 Lambda Literary Fellowship for nonfiction.

Miah is editor of the queer literary collaborative, Foglifter Press.

NOTHING KINKY

Evan McMurry

BOYLE STILL IN HIS FATIGUES screaming out of Fort Hood the moment they let him, like a rubber band yanked back ninety you-can't-believe-it straight days. Didn't even last an hour in his barracks-mate's borrowed GMC, crunching every pothole on I-35 with disregard for tires and earth, before pulling over at a restaurant that looked as though it would contain a long bar, which huzzah it did, where his ass met barstool with a *thwack* remembered by every employee and patron like an onside kick. He deducted one satisfying gulp from a perspiring Lone Star when his phone danced and base said some dumb motherfucker had crashed a jeep during training and blowed hisself to the other side, and who in the nation of Texas did Boyle think was going to clean that up, get back here. Boyle moped down his beer. "Fuck," he told it. "Can't even enjoy a fucking four-day."

New Millennium Writings, Issue 27, 2018

He felt the eyes of the 2 p.m. crowd on him, caressing him, wanting the uniform, some action, anything to stir-fuck their afternoon. "Can't even enjoy a fucking four-day!" he hollered with a slosh of the bottle that made him look drunk as he'd meant to get. And heeeeere comes the management.

Months later, well into his unsuccessful run at getting himself discharged, Boyle'd tell Yvette about the sun, how it burst through the front windows at an eager forty-five, hit the metal napkin dispenser on the far table and kept flying, banking off the mirror with the lunch specials scrawled in erasable marker above the bar, before finally brushing her cheek as she stepped nervously toward him. "That sun was *after* you," Boyle'd swear. "First I was like I'm on Team Sun because moment I saw you I knew I'd hop every surface to get to you too." He shifted in her twin bed. "But then I realized that sun was my competition."

"You proud 'cause you won?" Yvette moved atop him, moonlight sidling through her curtains and riding each rivulet of sweat from her temples to her torso, individual enough to be named.

Boyle stretched, long legs ending off her mattress edge. "If you're racing the sun," he said, "guess it helps that the sun sleeps."

Boyle did sleep, sort of, a zonked-out wakenap during which he shook and moaned and that left him more agitated in the morning, so that his spastic days seemed trials in venting the energy his body sparked in rest. What burned up his dreams? she asked. He couldn't remember, recalled only the panic. Yvette had terrors, too, according to anybody from her two brothers to previous boyfriends who'd had the apparent misfortune of sleeping beside her. "You angry," Server Todd told her on the last of their several regrettable nights. Said he'd woken up to her slapping him. He no-showed for his shift that day; Yvette had to do his opening duties. Heard later he'd up and moved to Dallas, as if she'd smacked him clear out of county. Sometimes she couldn't remember his name.

"Sir, we respect your service—" was how Yvette had started toward the tremolo soldier buzzing at her bar that Friday lunch shift. This still tickled her. She liked to repeat it when they were making love, Boyle perpendicular to her, hands grasping the back of her slick legs. "Sir, we respect your service," she'd giggle. He'd be unable to finish and she'd have to coax him out of the corner, pledging jest.

"Sir, we respect your service, it's just you can't cuss in the restaurant," she'd told him, her central Texas drawl making *rest-raunt* sound like the dual jingles of a shop door swinging open.

"Shit," he'd said, which he'd meant contrite. "I'm sorry, ma'am. It's just I was on leave and like that they're haulin' me back to the base."

"How long you on leave for?"

"Four days, was supposed to be."

"How long's it been so far?"

"Reckon it took me about forty minutes to get here?"

"Ooh." Now that was genuine, Boyle'd fight any soul in a hundred-mile radius said otherwise. That *ooh* echoed in his daydreams for the next three months until he floored it back to The Frontage Road. *Thwack* onto the stool. Yvette nearly sprinted over: "Would you guess it, I recognized the sound of you sitting down."

If that ain't love it'll do until. Yvette had never worried about anybody's tailbone before. She'd never thought about anybody's tailbone. Boyle offered to drive her out to Flynn's Dancehall, six miles down a ranch road; after stepping to some five-piece that owed Bob Wills royalties they wandered outside, and even under the star-poked sky and onto a picnic bench softened by rain and use, still his bony frame's end collided against the wood with a clap distinctive as voice. "Don't that *hurt*?" she asked him. His skin-pulled face looked up at her in wide wonderment. Man had no idea how he sat or did anything else. He was what Yvette's mother used to call an innocent. She knew to see behind force and profanity and all the rest. She divined who walked this earth meaning no crime. Boyle meant no crime.

Except literally. He wanted gone from the service, thought he'd figured a narrow opening through which he could offend enough to be booted without triggering any court martial. "War of attrition," he told her, shaky in his boast. Yvette knew his side of this war predated her, but now he had a cause beyond his own bald freedom, which he undervalued, on account of which he'd joined the service in the first place. "I was useless," he admitted. "That's what I told the recruitment guy at the mall who signed me up when he asked why I was joining. Guess what he said back? 'Knowing that makes you the smartest motherfucker in this mall and planet and whatever unit they put you in.' Didn't figure what he meant 'til too late."

Yvette's father still drove around town in a camouflage jeep with a black POW-MIA flag drooping over him at stoplights. He loathed war, loathed its corrosion, and like so many of that type his hate boiled into devotion. He read books on battles and planes and strategy and torture, wanting war endlessly, pleading for its shaping power; if all battles on this earth ended he'd brake in the middle of an intersection, causeless. It was up to his daughter to nudge it that last step and resist it all. In high school Yvette drew peace signs on her backpack with white out and ran her only pair of jeans through the wash with food coloring to try to make them tie-dye. Now the peace sign was implied: not for nothing was she the one dispatched to quiet the serviceman raising world war three at the bar at two in the afternoon. Sir, we appreciate your service.

"Ooh," she said when the soldier told her about his non-leave, and out of instinct ran her hand on his shoulder. He looked up and took her in, not how the lust-sodden did it down at the Gimme Three Steps but as if he, Boyle, specific knot of space and time in the great right-here-and-now, had never seen her like before and what the hell kind of world was *that*. Told her later he'd dreamt of her hand on his shoulder every night since, said he lulled himself to sleep by placing his own hand where hers had been.

Yvette had gone before to Flynn Hall with other guys but they stopped a couple numbers in as if having paid her entry fee and then got lousy off pitcher beer, so that she usually ended the night on some floor-mattress while sweaty hands tried to determine her breasts. Boyle, he danced all night, pausing once an hour to replenish his breath, and then he'd hear the stick-versus-stick of the drummer's countdown and clutch her hand, boyish to resume. That night Yvette was the one who sweated. Holding her outside after the dance hall closed, Boyle said she had a river down her back. She asked him to name it. Two-Step River, he said. Shuffle River. Quick-Quick Slow-Slow River. He swooped her swaying under moonlight as he babbled. Her hands cupped his poor tailbone.

Next day she was off work and he proposed driving, who cared where. In his borrowed truck they took a highway up 'til dirt. Northernmost Yvette had been was Amarillo. Beyond was Canada and cold and no-thank-you. Now she closed her eyes and let him guide her. They pulled up to a promontory looking out over Texas flat. The sun bent over their perch. Boyle told her he loved her and would marry her if it killed him. "If you're dead you can't dance, silly," she said, and he vowed to stay alive on behalf of their craft. They made love until exhausted and then dozed in the grass, both waking themselves with their own tremors, each rolling for solace into the other's sleeping form. Neither spoke of this but both found it stored in that extra drawer of consciousness two people can afford when they pool all their desires.

Then Boyle had to go back to base.

Meantime Yvette had *designs*, as the servers always put it when she was spotted studying a used anatomy textbook ahead of the lunch rush. Some new hostess being shown around, gawking at the textbook like it was a rock landed from space but why here. "Yvette's got designs. All wants to be a nurse. Not local, neither."

Guilty. Yvette had bussed down to Austin for cheer competitions junior and senior year. They didn't place but the city's glass buildings invited themselves into her mindscape and shone eternal. "More hospitals than you could count," some supplies salesman told her once of the capital city as she waited to scribble his order—all the lonely dick-dragged one-tops figured she was hourly for her conversation, and if she never served them a bite of well-done T-bone with extra A1 they'd starve past rapture. Yvette informed Mr. Salesman she intended to be a nurse. He presented her with his card, advised her, with a wink, to call him. She did not. His existence, up and down I-35 hawking gadgets to countless clinics that must have existed to buy them, was enough, and soon the corridor was a Mexico-to-Minnesota highway of hospitals breathless for her. Yeah, she studied.

Yvette told Boyle her plans in letters (his phone privileges had been revoked as one rolling consequence of his discharge mission), her first letters since she'd been forced to write in careful kid script to her father's hermetic mother in one of the two Carolinas. Now she penned pages, at the iced tea station after her sidework had been signed off on, when she awoke in the light-yellow crevice of early morning before sliding back to sleep. She filled in her fantasies with detail and certitude she'd never permitted her own imagination. Her daydreams grew bones and flesh, stood on their own hind legs and strode off to Austin, to an apartment together, a gig for him pouring concrete paying more than you'd think, the ring on her finger thin and near unnoticeable, but lord in the right summer sunray you'd have to shield your eyes from Lubbock.

Boyle's handwriting back was as she expected, wild scratches and loops, like her dinner orders, jotted in jagged code meant for the line cooks forced to learn it. She spent hours crowbarring apart and reassembling his script. He agreed in frantic hand to all her plans and then boosted them, promising to procure two jobs at least so they could buy a by-god house out in Bastrop where there's LAND, with three underlines indenting from alternating angles, as if he were already crisscrossing his someday acreage. Boyle begged her forgiveness for joining the service that now encased him from her and warped their future, though, his rambling letter demurred, were it not for his uniform would Yvette have even noticed him, would he have even been in The Frontage Road that afternoon hooting and hollering? Was it not this very same service, by calling him back, that called her to him? *That's a cruel loop!* he wrote, though it looked like *thank acwolmpl* until she decrypted it.

The letters became less frequent as his discharge mission cost him additional privileges. Finally Yvette wondered at the flaw in his scheme: if he continued his mischief, wouldn't they eventually refuse to let him off base at all? Wouldn't the ultimate punishment be not discharge but capture? This was their sole fight, conducted via post, her side inked on the back of pink food delivery carbons, his on printer paper swiped from chaplain's office. Was he really willing to sacrifice those few days with her? she demanded. Boyle asked if she wanted him for four days now or forever later. She wrote back: both. *Ain't no both*, replied the thrice-folded page. *Can only kick around here so long 'til they ship me out. Believe it they're shipping folk.*

The surge she saw about on the TV. No thank you. Yvette began adding peace signs next to her name when she dropped the check, the way the other female servers drew hearts and the male servers drew nothing. In late bleak howl-hours she turned morose, loading troop death counts, touring the war porn some deathwish third-tours uploaded to message boards, tank marks impressed in skulls because in some streets were stacked too many bodies to move them out of the way. Yvette closed the browsers, curled up with Boyle's letters and visions of Austin and tailbone ailments memorized from her textbook. Applications had been mailed to nursing schools down in the 512, responses maybe some day.

She shook awake from nightmares, dawn's fingers crossed in her east-facing windows, refreshed the news to see if the war had expired while her eyes had closed from it.

Finally a letter arrived. Boyle said he'd been a downright boy scout and salvaged his next four-day. Two weeks until he got loose. One week. Four days. Tomorrow.

Now that she knew he'd be coming she heard the *thwack* of his rear against stool before it happened, as if the two of them travelled faster than sound, the sluggish world banging and tumbling to keep up. He spun in his seat as she closed out her last tables, held her hand tenderly out the door, chauffeuring her to their together-realm so fast she forgot to run her checkout and the manager called her after midnight because the POS system wouldn't shut down with her open tabs.

Boyle wanted her to meet his mom, mused this as he drove dance hall-bound, though he admitted in almost the same breath the woman was crabby and lotto-hung and would probably be short with her but didn't mean it personally.

"Daddy'd be obsessed with you," Yvette countered. "He thinks soldiers are tragic. He'd salute you and at the same time be ranting about them Ivy League puppetmasters conned us into Vietnam. Seen him do it. He forgets to take his hand down from his head, sometimes. I have to move it for him."

Boyle swerved one-handed into the hall's sandy lot. "I'm not tragic."

"Daddy'd say not yet."

They won a dance competition that night, $200 prize, plus every old coot couple in the place wanted to buy them a round because they'd never seen such love since their own. Some of the men had their veteran caps on, brigades stitched in yellow. Sniffed soldier on Boyle a mile out, started right in with their stories, because why had they seen and suffered what they had if not to tell. Yvette would extract him each time for a new number. The old men, they went home early. Boyle and Yvette drank hooch with the band after last call, stumbled back along the dark road's gravel embankment. The nightblack routed Boyle's joy and he collapsed despondent in her bedroom. "Never want to be them guys," he cried. "Uh-uh. Never never never." She cradled him until he fell asleep, L-shaped on the floor against her bed, twitching.

But in the morning they had $200 and three days of self-rule. Yonder was an antique strip, doily stores piled with garden gnomes, LBJ plates, flash-bulb cameras bought at garage sales repriced for gouging. Some of those shops sold jewelry, some of that jewelry were rings, and $200 turned out to be just enough for one ruby-colored gemstone a haughty woman behind the counter warned could be soft as butter so y'all *watch*. Boyle slid it onto Yvette's ring finger. "Watch this," he murmured, just loud enough for the antique woman to hear and huff and manners these days. Yvette was already lifting her ring into the pouring sun, probably blinding some Lubbock fool.

Now they were near broke, but who needed money. They made love until noon, testing different positions, still discovering each other's bodies, Boyle slanting her up against her white childhood dresser, Yvette blindfolding him with her single knit scarf it was never cold enough to wear, Boyle finding the exact point of his cock against her clit that solicited that *ooh* that had first melted him. For a euphoric cross-moment that sound and this one were joined, as if their hunger for each other was so powerful time twisted around to bear witness.

Loved out, they scrounged loose change from her lunch tips and nibbled on scones at the town's one coffee shop, penciling in half-finished crossword puzzles left by the sugar, reading personal ads aloud from the back of the free weekly and imagining answering them. "Husband seeks man to have sex with his pregnant wife while he watches," Yvette recited. "Nothing kinky."

"No way it says that."

She proved it. He howled. So pristine they booked it home and made love in roaring celebration. Yvette stuck her finger up his ass until he whooped "Nothing kinky!!!!!!!!" loud enough that her downstairs neighbor banged something dense against his ceiling. Became their joke: they treated themselves to pizza on the third night, Yvette asking what he wanted on it, Boyle saying, "Pepperoni, olives. Nothing kinky." The morning he had to drive back, Boyle asking the weather, Yvette answering, "30% change of rain, nothing kinky."

His next four-day was three months away. "I'll behave," he swore, twining two fingers. "Boy scout." Boyle asked if three months was time enough to book a venue, a gazebo in the park or something. "You, me, your dad, my mom. Who-all else. Some of your friends. I could get a couple of guys at base to drive down."

Yvette hadn't yet cried at his leaving, but she did now. "Don't need no venue," she said, choking on the words. "Just you and me."

"And the pregnant woman's husband. He wants to watch."

"Forget him." Yvette sniffled, wiped her cheeks. She pledged to be dirty as could be on their wedding night, naughtiness unheard of, so filthy they'd kick her out of the solar system. "Well don't do *that*," Boyle said, honestly concerned. "Horrible things we'll do to each other," she promised, twisting the ring new enough it still itched. Her eyes watered but she grinned through. "Set your clock, boy. In ninety days I'll shock you something."

"Okay," Boyle agreed, sideways-grinning as though slipping through a gap in his base's gates, "but nothing kinky."

They shipped him out two weeks later. Yvette was mid-lunch rush, one of the line cooks having called in sick so the place a cluster, didn't see the blinking light on her phone until hours later. He'd begged phone privileges back for this one call, said his static-y voicemail. "Plus I reckon they feel bad for me. Like, better give the cannon fodder his phone call. Ha ha." That laugh snare-drummed over her ear. She saved the message, listened to it over the next weeks, and then months, learning to cut it off right before his death rattle.

A couple letters arrived long after they were written, about the barracks and the missions, how much he missed her, and what the fuck was he doing here. Then nothing. They never married and she wasn't kin—she reckoned nobody at the base even knew she existed—so nobody knew to tell Yvette anything. She saw about him in the base newsletter somebody'd left behind at one of her booths, a listing of the most recent KIA. *Boyle Wren of South Pass, Georgia, 21.* Just long enough to read over his name in a typewriter's tombstone print before the kitchen bell brrrringed, order up. She stuffed the notice in her apron pouch; it rode there rest of the shift, stole home with her, joining his letters, some mismatched tube socks left at her place, and her ring, all she had of him. We thank you for your service.

That night her legs kicked in her twin bed. She wanted to go dancing with him. All she'd imagined she'd feel the few times she'd allowed herself to ponder this end, not in a million had Yvette ever thought it would make her want to two-step. Felt godless, except Boyle would have loved it. This dream tricked her into sleep, where her petition for him to reconsider his discharge mission scaled her memory and charged. She started awake, sky still black, reread his letter in the lamplight, *ain't no both* scrawled in warning script. She vomited onto her pillow.

At daylight she called in sick to The Frontage Road, hung up as the manager bleated about how we get our shifts covered round here. Didn't bother phoning the next two days. One server eventually texted: *How them designs*?

Her father was the first other person Yvette saw, on her sixth jobless day of roving in and out of sleep on her closet floor to avoid her unwashed sheets. In his black-draped jeep he ordered her a chicken sandwich at a drive-thru, shared a basket of fries in the parking lot. He catalogued, in that gruff, weary, keep-on-keeping-on voice of his, the endless waste in Iraq, lies from official lecterns, articles he'd read of soldiers returning with whole regions of their skulls bolted together, and them the lucky ones. As usual he spoke beyond her, all the centuries of conflagration imminent in his windshield like those old wall-wide paintings in which every gun and cannon of a battle explodes at once. He didn't ask her nothing, didn't notice her ring, her matted hair, her hard swallow as he told of the men who came back. He offered Yvette the final handful of fries—"small things, Vette, in times like this," he said of his gesture, "and let's remember the ones who die for it"—then dropped her back at her apartment, where she earned an eviction that afternoon for torching her sheets in the complex's dumpster.

Yvette moved to Austin the next week. Picked up some shifts at a diner way north on Burnet Road, enough takehome to rent a room in a too-crowded house where her training scrubs eventually earned her the nickname Nurse Ratchet from roommates who told her she shrieked in her sleep. Oranges and reds from their backyard campfires defied her curtains as she dug a fingernail into the flesh of her thumb to stay awake. In nightmares the tank rolled over Boyle's head, Yvette screaming for them to move his body. She offered to pay more in rent for her noise; the roommates, scared of her, told her it was fine and she endured their shifting glances in the hallway.

And lord did men hit on her, at her nursing program, on the bus, hoofing down the streets she'd once dreamed of striding with Boyle. She'd exhibit her ring but it was dim and powerless, just some thrift store find. Yvette learned to slap, just as with server what's-his-name. The boys jerked back stunned, like a prowling beast encountering an electric fence indifferent to food chain etiquette. "Bitch," they'd squeal. Sure, she'd shrug, ring finger extended, hoped they told that part at a pub later, cunt didn't even know which finger you gave.

Eventually the roughage did begin to scratch the stone, as the antique woman had warned.

But Yvette chased the sun's swoop off the band. Exact angle? Sun could catch that ring, tell you what. See it out there in Lubbock. See it in the Frontage Road, it in Gimme Three Steps, at Flynn's Dancehall, way out at Fort Hood, curse the place, see it up there in Amarillo, all the way up

I-35 in Minnesota, see it in Canada and cold and no-thank-you. Exactly how Boyle had swore, testifying of first laying eyes on her. They were picnicking on that promontory he'd been told about from the same guy who'd leant him the GMC. The sun setting across a panorama laid out special reminded Boyle of that instant she'd appeared to him. "Man, that sun hit off every surface hunting for you. I counted three. At least. Would have kept going. That's how you do," he'd said, tremolo soldier peering up at her, meaning nothing but this worship, meaning pure. "Like the sun. Girl, every goddamn surface after you."

Writing Advice, NMW 2018

Every story has its own logic, and one of the keys I've discovered to writing is first finding and then being smart enough to follow that logic. Often the story will want to go back and forth through time, or make leaps in points of view, in ways that would seem to violate writing orthodoxy. The orthodoxy shouldn't be discarded—it's there for a reason, and when you cross it you need to recompense the reader some other way to keep them from being ejected from the world you're creating.

But ultimately, the rules can be bent to fit the story. If you know your characters well enough, they will lead you.

Evan McMurry

New Millennium
Award for Fiction

"Nothing Kinky"

Evan McMurry's fiction has been published in more than a dozen journals, including *Post Road, Euphony, Arcturus, Oddville Press, Palaver,* and more. His story, "The Fall of Rabbi Gold," was selected as a finalist for the Al-Simāk Award for Fiction from the Chicago Review of Books.

MAPPING HANA

Cassady Black

THE NIGHT BEFORE MY WIFE DISAPPEARED, she turned to me at twilight and said, *I have unruly thoughts*. I hoped she was referring to me, and the fact that our two-year-old daughter was sound asleep at an unusually early hour after a long afternoon garden party celebrating my parents' fiftieth anniversary. I moved toward my wife, Hana, and ran my hands down the back of her red party dress. I remember that she did not shiver and withdraw from my touch that night the way she had begun to do so often that summer.

But that last night in our home in Boulder in late August was different. Hana came to me willingly, right there on our patio, lifting her dress and climbing up on my lap. I don't remember that she smiled during any of this, but a man starved for affection could easily overlook that fact. She looked as beautiful to me as she did the night that I had first met her in Barcelona ten years earlier, even though for quite some time she had taken to changing her look every few months without explanation. She straddled me and kissed me with her full red lips, the one part of her body she had not yet tried to alter. She wore the same lipstick every single day, even when she was in her eating-nachos-for-breakfast phase. There were often lipstick tubes of the shade called Burnished Rose to be found in bathrooms and cars, and somehow this stability reassured me. She didn't say anything to me that last night as we made love—not a word, not the murmur of my name, Michael, not even a small sigh—but I looked in her eyes and she was right there for me.

No matter what everyone else says now, over a year after her disappearance, no matter how often it is suggested to me that if my wife isn't dead she has to be crazy and it's not my fault, I believe that none of these things can possibly be true.

I make a living as a futurist, studying the past and predicting trends, but as often as I studied my own wife day by day, there was not a single moment when I could have imagined what was to come in my own life. Granted, she did call herself "Zelda" occasionally, but only in sandwich-shops and other places that ask for your first name so that they can call it out when your order is ready. *My name is Zelda*, she would say in her deep, soft voice, without laughing, as though it were true. I would stand by her side and feel not crazy, but younger, stronger, more capable in my own life because I was married to a woman with such spark and imagination. I never acted like a normal husband and asked her why she did this—perhaps it would have been a good idea to have done so.

Today there is a woman on Pearl Street who looks nothing like Hana but yet could be. I have to check. It has become my favorite pastime, overtaking my previous passion for collecting antique maps. I consider what to say if I see my wife somewhere in my travels, contemplating trick questions in case she looks completely different and denies her identity. I couldn't explain this to the private detective I hired back in the beginning, but I can almost imagine what Hana is capable of if she doesn't want to be found. *You need to use more imagination, Michael,* she would say to me so often. *The future has to have crystal trains and emerald rains and things that may never come true.*

I think I would still know her anywhere, but how can I identify someone who I could barely describe month to month even when I was living with her? She came into my life with long dark hair and a trim body. At one time or another she went through many colors: she became a redhead, a blond, then back to black and now who knows what. She went through body types too: a buff athlete, a matronly looking woman carrying an extra twenty pounds, a skinny raver with a pierced navel. She was getting thinner and thinner when she disappeared. I never said much, because it was mildly entertaining, in an offbeat, unpredictable way.

I let the detective go after a while, and then the police lost interest in the case. "There are all kinds of spouses who voluntarily vanish every day," they told me, "and it's not illegal for adults to run away from home. Let us know if anything concrete turns up." There will be nothing to let them know, of this I am sure. But I am also sure from my studies that there are patterns in people that do not change. If I can remember the things that were true about Hana, I can identify where she is going and when she will arrive.

The woman on Pearl Street is about five foot seven, which is the right height, and her lips are painted a deep red. She is on rollerblades, wearing black shorts and a black sports bra, with her dark blond hair clipped short. I do not ask every woman with red lips if she is my wife, only certain ones, and I think it is a kind of energy, a magnetic life force, that compels me to check certain women. Up close, I can see that this woman is probably not more than twenty-five, but she does have a string of yellow dandelions woven through the side of her hair. I am not kind. I say the name of Hana's long-dead father, a name she never willingly used. I watch the eyes for a flicker of recognition or shock.

"Excuse me, miss? Did you ever know a dead soldier named Edward Granville?"

No shock, no interest beyond looking me up and down quickly to see if I might be anyone who matters.

"Never heard of him," she says. "Sorry." Then she pauses and begins to smile at me, the way women smile at me now, because I am obviously a sad and confused man. I could keep talking to her, I could tell her my story and maybe she'd come home with me and keep me warm, but there are too many ways to be lonely with a complete stranger in your bed.

She tells me she's an instructor at Naropa; I tell her my name—*nice to meet you, Michael Augustine*—I buy her a coffee, but I do not yet tell her anything interesting. She thinks predicting the future is fascinating, so I ask her my standard question of people I meet: "When you close your eyes and see the end of this century in 2099, what one thing do you imagine will be new and different?" It's cheap research but good conversation. Very few people have the vision to consider the reality of such a long span, but Hana always did. She knew history, she knew literature, she understood. She could make up something new and interesting every single day. *There will be no marriage,* she'd say. *It's outdated. Only ten-year renewable contracts, but with lifetime commitments to children.* She would tell me her strange dreams and then suggest that dreams were the future. *There will be festivals that last an entire year, in which people dance and dream themselves into future rituals for their society. Do you know, Michael, that there is an Australian aboriginal tribe that does this? The Kunapipi festival goes on for thirty years, an entire generation. They perform a part of it each year and at the end they have determined their future lives for the next sixty years.*

"I know who you are, Professor Augustine," the dandelion girl says after a long pause. "You're the professor whose wife disappeared into thin air. Everybody knows your story. I'm sorry."

"Thanks."

Of course. Everybody feels sorry for me, everybody knows, hardly anyone ever mentions it anymore. I am fully aware that I am the pity-fuck of three cities where I work, here and abroad. My parents won't even speak Hana's name. As far as they're concerned, their granddaughter has no mother, and they tend to treat me like I'm not in the best of health.

This woman is definitely not Hana, but she is very alive. "I think," she says, smiling at the rise of her own imagination, smiling at me in that flirting way that so many women do, a smile that suggests that maybe she's the woman who can save me, "that in the future women will be in charge of the world. Men will have to wait for women to call them for dates, and maybe even dress in high heels for work."

I let her take me home after all. She is young, she is energetic, and her apartment is filled with flowers. She humors me by applying the fresh lipstick I request, and with her deep red lips she leaves her mark on my body as she tries so very hard to make me a happy man.

Hana holds a Master's degree in literature; she could recite long segments of Molly Bloom's sexual soliloquy by heart and often did late at night when I asked her to—*yes and his heart was going like mad and yes I said yes I will yes*—she wrote travel articles for a living; she was kind; she catered to my every sexual whim for a very long time. She was surprised to become pregnant, surprised to be a mother, but she took to it after a while. I could be practical, that's easy to come by. Hana could get right down on the floor and make up stories and imaginary games just like kids do. She could build with blocks and play with dolls for hours and actually enjoy it. But for a month after the birth she wouldn't name the baby, *just like some native tribes do*, she told me, *they let the child grow into their own name.*

Then one morning she said at breakfast, *I had a dream. We have to name her Layla. I met Eric Clapton once when I was a teenager and he kissed me.* It wasn't quite like picking an old family name, but it was a nice name and I was relieved to have any name for our child. Layla Granville Augustine would have a bright future.

There were days when I would walk quietly out of my study, stand in the doorway of the bathroom and watch Hana and Layla cavort together in their bubble bath surrounded by plastic bath toys. Two beautiful nude female forms, one so tiny and one barely grown-up, playing together. I sometimes thought I should hire an artist to come draw a portrait of them exactly that way, and now I wish I had. Hana was a good mother, no matter what anyone else says, and in some ways she still is.

There are 49 framed maps in my house, all of them valuable. It's possible that this is why Hana ever agreed to marry me. In my work, I teach, speak, consult and write about past and future trends for the public and for private companies. In order to be a successful futurist, I have to be an optimist—nobody wants to hear that the future is bleak. And in order to be an optimist and still live in this world, I have to focus on beauty and memory and a certain kind of history. The maps on my walls create a vision for anyone who enters my home, an illusion of security and the meaning of time and space, not unlike entering a church. The first time Hana entered the great room when I brought her back from Barcelona she stopped and sat down cross-legged on the deep gray carpet. She looked around at the room that contains nothing but a circular couch and walls lined with individually lit maps, nodded in approval at me and whispered, *So many people lack their own brand of joy.*

She didn't take a dime from our joint accounts when she left, so I let the police assume foul play and work on hunting her down. I tried to imagine both the best and the worst, but when a woman crawls into bed with you at 11:00 p.m. and is not there when you wake up in the morning, it's hard to imagine much foul play. I assumed she was hiding somewhere, and I didn't even report her missing for almost two days. She often got up at 2:00 a.m. to dye or cut her hair, or to clean out her wardrobe, sometimes muttering to herself—*is it beautiful? Is it moral? Is it true?* And then would come back to bed a different person. She didn't take her suitcase when she left, and I can't tell quite what might be missing of her clothes. I still haven't moved anything out of the closets. Layla often plays beneath her mother's clothes, sitting in the middle of the shoes. I only know that my wife went to bed next to me completely naked that night and in the morning there was nothing but space where she had been.

Hana often traveled, so it wasn't unusual for her to be gone. I didn't start making up stories for Layla for a week or so. We had a good nanny and housekeeper, so having Hana gone was not that difficult in a practical way, only in spirit. "Layla," I told her on day ten when there were no goodnight phone calls to her and she began to wonder, "Mama's had to go on a trip. She's in…" I paused, walking toward the four maps on Layla's bedroom wall and pointing at a region colored bright red, ready to make up anything. "She's in…" Layla was only two years old but loved her maps and knew them well. "Wonderland!" she said in that precious little voice. I had pointed to the map of fictional lands on her wall and located her mother not too far from Alice and the White Rabbit.

We changed her location often—Hana got to travel to Narnia, to the Lion City of Africa and spent at least a month in Never Never Land. While she was there she did fantastic things, often saving people from misery and bringing grand presents for children. I was required to dig for imagination I didn't know I had every time I went to kiss my daughter goodnight.

We had Hana pinpointed as arriving in the Land of Fabled Flowers on the bedroom map the night that Layla showed me the first note. She pulled a postcard out from under her pillow and told me that she and the nanny had retrieved it from the mailbox that day. It was a photograph of a bright red hummingbird, flying across a body of water labeled as the Gulf of Mexico. It had a stamp, but no postmark, almost as though someone had walked by the house and dropped it off. Layla's name and our address were carefully printed on the back, and the message half of the postcard only had the word "HOPE" in bold print, circled by a penciled-in design that filled up all the rest of the white space.

It could have come from anyone.

Memory haunts me. I am in Barcelona when the new millennium begins. I am thirty-three, Hana is twenty-three and does not yet know that I exist. She stands chatting and laughing with her friend, Marissa, in the gallery directly in front of the map I want to see. She wears a white sundress, her long black hair flowing to the middle of her back. I am tall, with my longish brown hair pulled back in a ponytail, wearing a tweed sports coat. I like to think I am sophisticated and worldly, but I know in my heart that even with contact lenses women still think I'm a guy who reads too much, a man old before his time who wanders museums and art galleries because he has no other life. Hana Granville looks smart, she looks sexy, she looks available, and she becomes a part of my erotic vision of ancient Mesopotamia that looms behind her on the map. I am alone in Spain and unruly thoughts are not uncommon to me in my lonely nights.

I summon up all the charm I've ever imagined, introduce myself, and attempt to impress the girls with my knowledge of the map. We drink a lot of champagne. She comes back to my flat with her friend. They watch me light the candles, and as I start to pour some wine Hana says, *I came home with you because you look like a picture I have of my father when he was in Vietnam in 1969.* I turn to offer her a drink while I consider what to say, and she is standing up and slipping the white strap of her dress off of her shoulder. *You look like my father,* she repeats, dropping the dress down to her ankles and stepping out of it, standing before me completely nude, offering herself as a gift.

There may be a proper etiquette for what to do when a woman you've known for four hours drops her dress on your floor while her girlfriend looks on, but I don't know what that might be. I laugh nervously. Marissa lounges back on my couch looking slightly bored and not at all amused. Marissa is tall with short black hair and not unattractive, but she does not hold my interest tonight.

"Your father?" I repeat, and Hana shrugs and smiles innocently at me. I take her hand. There is nothing else to do. I lead her to my bed that is at least behind a screen, and I lay her down and begin to hear the poetry of my youth—*somewhere I have never traveled, gladly beyond any experience.*

At some point during the night I hear Marissa snoring on my couch; at some point during the night Hana reaches for me and calls me *Daddy;* at that point I transform beyond my own recognition and am inspired to perform in ways that I never thought possible.

A trend identified years later: in the morning, Hana is rational, charming and bright, and it is almost as though I was with a different woman last night. The chaperone on the couch is gone.

I am only half-crazy, she tells me right up front over late morning coffee, and if this is half-crazy then I am ready to be right there with her. She tells me the story of her life in one long monologue; I watch her red lips and believe every word she says.

Half-crazy, she says, *means I was diagnosed with what they call cyclothymia, a minor and polite version of manic-depression. I call it baby bi-polar these days. Sometimes I do crazy and impulsive things, like last night, but I always come back sooner or later and I never actually harm anyone. My mother was probably the same, but people didn't know as much about it back then. I was born in San Francisco and my mother had a hard time there. My father died from alcoholism, and when I was a three-year-old kid, my mother jumped off the Golden Gate Bridge. But she survived—some people do, you know. Maybe it's luck, maybe fate. We moved to London to live with my aunt and everyone thought my mother would be okay, but she was hit by a bus and died when I was ten. My aunt sent me through school, and now I'm traveling and writing poetry.*

She offers all of this as a matter-of-fact history, so I hold her hand and say I'm sorry about her parents. It's possible I'm the most boring man on earth, but I give her my story next anyway—normal parents, two sisters, too much education, good work, an old Victorian house with a private walled garden and an urge to start living my real life. I can at least talk about the future to sound vaguely interesting, so I tell her one of my pet theories—that when researchers find out more about the genetic markers for depression and other related "psychological" diseases in the near future, the concepts of "sin" and "evil" as we know them will disappear.

"There will be reasons for everything, Hana, there always are. People like Hitler, or even common criminals, will be medically diagnosed. We'll be able to scientifically say what was wrong with them, trace it back through their families, and know for a fact what caused their brand of 'evil.' There aren't many 'normal' people in the world, as far as I can tell. Perhaps everyone will be tested and diagnosed for mental illnesses as a child, and maybe inoculated, not unlike chicken pox. Can you imagine?"

I don't know, she says quietly. *Maybe all the art would disappear. You know what they say—in darkness the true artist paints.*

Most of the time I loved her moods. It didn't matter to me—she would get melancholic some days, and I would hold her tight until the tears disappeared. She would move to crazy laughter and brilliant sanity and do impulsive things on other days, and I adored every minute of it. She wrote ecstatic poetry and performed it for me in the wee hours of the morning. This was not a bad way to live. I often envied her.

I pried her away from Marissa and brought her home to Boulder with me. I found a photograph in her closet of the three of us in Barcelona and I've hung it on the wall. I look thrilled, Hana looks lost, and Marissa looks like her usual unamused self. After we were married, Hana didn't think she wanted children and I didn't really care, but it only took one impulsive night on a trip to San Francisco, no birth control, and the future changed again.

One night when Layla was still a baby, Hana woke up in the middle of the night and began to pace the house nude, pausing to write things down every now and then. I asked her why she was up at that hour. *Because, Michael,* she said gently, as though I were a child who knew very little of how the world worked. *Because sometimes at 3:00 a.m. words begin to circle down, falling like snow, melting where they land, disappearing into the night.*

She was so beautiful at that moment and I knew there was something I should do for her, but all I wanted was to take her back to bed and make hard, fast love to her. "Come back to bed, baby."

Michael, I am inventing words. I keep lists. 'Nutaryuk' is what the Eskimos say for fresh snow—'aniu, qanuk, natquik,' dozens of words for almost the same thing because it is so very important. Words matter. My favorite Eskimo word is 'qanisqineq'—snow floating on water. I think I will invent a hundred words for hope, she whispered, *maybe one for hope falling gently and then hope rising in the absence of words, hope against reason, and hope for fragile hearts.*

Besides the picture with Marissa, I found 12 different pictures of Hana, had them framed and put them on the wall. "In the bathroom," insisted Layla, so she could splash in the bubbles and look at her missing mother at night, chattering to her all the time. This bath is on the third floor of our old house and I've made sure that nobody else sees it but myself and my daughter, as though it is unhealthy to have a shrine to the missing woman who changed your life. Layla has collected all of her mother's lipstick tubes and we use them as little submarines in the bathtub. We both feel safe in that room, and after she's cleaned up, Layla kisses one of her mama's pictures goodnight before she goes to bed. I do the same.

Late one night there is a phone call. It is after midnight when it wakes me up. *I am disenchanted with dreams,* the woman's voice says. *Please keep your eyes closed for me.*

What wouldn't I do for this voice? She tells me an erotic story, she tells me how she is touching herself and she tells me to do the same. I do. In the morning I realize I was half-asleep and it could have been anyone—maybe one of the women who think I'm so "eligible," or maybe a college girl on a prank. It might even have been a waking dream. Or, it could simply have been a wrong number.

There are angels in the architecture, spinning in infinity, the song says, and perhaps it is true. It has always been possible that Hana is at the bottom of the lake, or that she left to follow her mother's footsteps toward a high bridge. But there are feelings that circle down around me at 3:00 a.m. and at those moments I can predict that this is not true.

I receive an email from Marissa, saying she will be in Denver and wants to meet me for lunch. I haven't seen her in almost eight years, although she and Hana kept in touch. I spoke to her several times after Hana disappeared. She knew nothing.

"The only thing I never told you, Michael," she says over lunch, "is that Hana did call me the week before she left. *There is nothing I will miss from this century,* she told me, and I assumed she was talking about all the new technology or something."

"Was she unhappy?"

Marissa laughs. "Who knows, with Hana? One day she would be, one day not, you know how she is. I don't know, Michael, I really don't know what happened—you knew she was crazy when you met her, you took your chances."

"Only half-crazy. What's your best guess?" I stare at Marissa across the lunch table, the same way that I stare at all women these days. It occurs to me that if Marissa wasn't so tall, even she could be Hana in disguise.

"Maybe she had a whole new identity for all those looks she tried on, and you weren't paying attention. Or maybe she met someone else. A man. Or a woman. Who knows?"

"A woman?"

Marissa raises her eyebrows and I can tell she's going to say something that gives her a certain amount of pleasure. "Surely you know that Hana and I were lovers before you took her away from me? We were going to travel around the world together. Then you stepped in."

"No, she never told me. Never." What else didn't she tell me? Should I have somehow known this? "That first night in Barcelona, when you stayed—what was that all about?"

She shrugs. "You looked like her father, Michael. She told you that. What could I do? I didn't know you, so I stayed to protect her in some passive way. But you had money and stability, you looked like her father and you were dying to take care of her. I couldn't compete with any of that."

"I did take care of her. For ten years."

"I know."

There is silence as we consider all the things that we don't know.

"But!" Marissa says with forced brightness to break the mood, "I brought pictures for you. I was cleaning out my studio, and found these, I thought you might want them, or maybe some day when Layla is grown up she might want them."

A large brown portfolio is handed across the table and I open it to find a dozen nude photographs of Hana, exactly as she was the year that I met her. She is soft, she is beautiful, she is alive.

"She was my model, you know. This set of photos I called my own 'blue nudes.' She would never let me use them and I can't do anything with them now."

I knew nothing, only the apparent few things that Hana chose to tell me. I can not take my eyes off of the photographs. Everything in the background is some shade of blue, contrasting with Hana's white skin. She is laughing in one picture, her head tilted to the side, black wavy hair flowing down her shoulders on to her bare breasts, and she is looking directly at the camera with a look of surprise. The look reaches right through me.

There are paths that a man can take to get where he wants to be. Not long after the lunch with Marissa, I send all of the nude photos of my young wife over to a friend to be blown up to wall-size posters. I hang them on the walls in the attic, away from prying eyes, away from sunlight, but not away from my drawings in the dark of night.

The blue backgrounds become like bodies of water—oceans of curtains, flowing rivers of chairs, lakes of softly draped blue velvet material. I begin with one picture, drawing my route up

Hana's leg with my pen, up over her bent knee, carefully labeling it as the route to where the Colorado River begins. The mount of her right breast becomes Grand Lake, her belly is the beginning of Trail Ridge Road. I will map each place that I have been with Hana, one place meticulously drawn on each bare body—Barcelona, San Francisco, Hawaii, Vancouver, London, and more. I will map our own house, our own garden. I will use light for each map as required, including candlelight for Barcelona. If I study a good map long enough, I can often determine the forces in place during its creation.

The future is mine. There will be more notes and calls and I am almost sure it will be her. There may be something I have forgotten to do. There are things I can say when I get another chance, and I must determine what they are. She had something important to do, some place that required her presence, or maybe there was some place she simply could not be. Perhaps the rest of this century will be a better place for her to be located. It is entirely possible that on any particular evening, Hana will walk up the driveway, check the mail, and when I come home I will find her upstairs in the bathtub with Layla.

The issue is one of time, and space. I will travel until I find her there.

NEW MILLENNIUM
AWARD FOR FICTION

“Mapping Hana”

Cassady Black lives in Colorado, where she is a writer, editor, and consultant. She is a founding editor of ***Slow Trains Literary Journal*** (slowtrains.com), and her writing has been published in ***Eclectica***, ***Salon.com***, and ***The Best American Erotica series***, among others.

cassadyblack.com

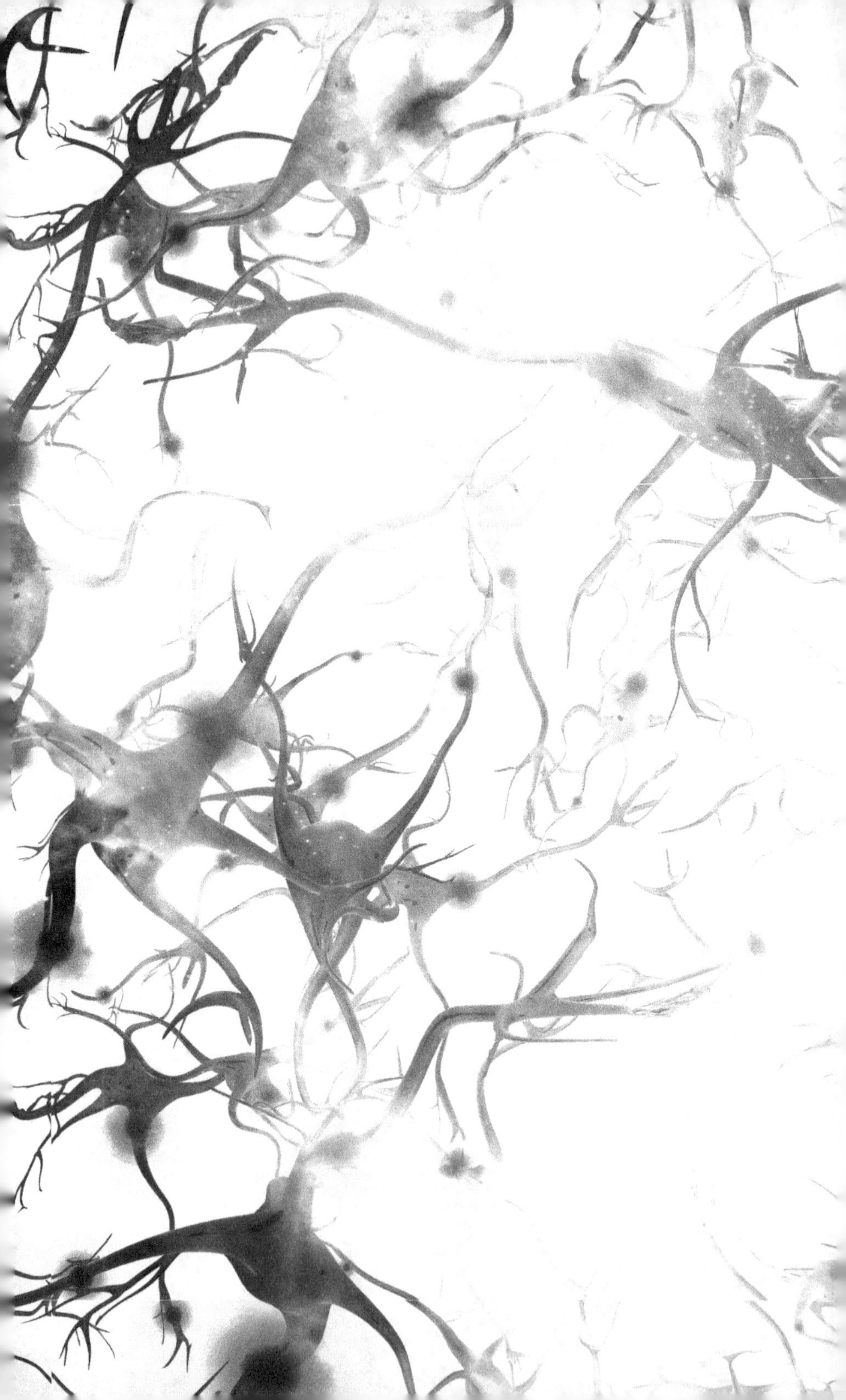

DENDRITES

Anne Gudger

Before.

When you were stardust.

When you were in between your last life and this.

When your particles dipped and tangoed.

When the space in your atoms was infinite.

When you looked around and said, "That family. That one." Because your soul wanted healing. Because you knew you'd learn a type of love with them.

Stardust. Ether. Twilight.

The in-between.

Between then and now. Now and next.

New Millennium Writings, Issue 27, 2018

Will you hold it in your weathered hand?

Glitter light cradled in your girl hands, billowing in, out like you were playing your mom's concertina as the light ball shrunk and grew from watermelon to cantaloupe to plum and back. Light arced between your palms, sizzling with fuzzy edges. Light bulb white. Blue white. Rainbow white. Shimmer between your fingers too when you spread them wide, when you squinted at the in-between space when you saw light webs like glass fibers that tickled your skin.

You didn't know everyone didn't see it until one kindergarten day, home from school, in your flannel nightgown with the frayed hem from worrying it, flopped on the nubby couch, orange juice and a thermometer on the coffee table. Your mom in black slacks and a pressed white blouse half way up a metal ladder, washing the Taller Than Her living room windows. The smell of vinegar tickled your nose. The squeak of crumpled newspaper as she dried the glass, her arm swinging in half circles. The madrona tree out the windows with its peely bark and soft underside, with its burnt orange berries the birds would eat then crash into the picture windows.

"Look, Mama," you said and held your hands out, palms up, the light between them electric.

"What?" she said, pushing her wavy black bangs with the heel of her hand.

"See?" you tried again and raised your hands, that rainbow lifting with you.

"See what?" she said and scrunched her brow, her worry look. She peeled off lemon yellow rubber gloves and climbed down the ladder that dug its feet deeper into carpet. And, "Let me take your temperature."

When you're an adult, you'll walk into a rock shop in Montana, smell dust and dry. You'll love the agates and their dendrites caught in rock. As you palm the agates, trace the little tree dendrites with your finger, you'll remember this day. Flopped on the couch. The first time of many when you understood that what comes through to you doesn't come through to everyone. You'll squeeze your eyes and conjure this childhood memory. You'll wish you could reach back to your young self and say, *Look at the light in your hands. How beautiful it is. Keep playing with it as it sizzles and sparks and stretches.*

Instead the veil between here and there thickened.

Dad with Vodka coffee. Mom with Self Help books, becoming a line drawing of herself. Their crazy divorce.

The light in your girl hands dimmed as the veil grew a shell—thin as crackling fall frost, thick as the Missouri River frozen in winter.

Twenty-eight and pregnant. Your love cup overflowed and all that love and trust thinned the veil again. Intuition, people say. You were glad yours was turned back up. You hugged your husband long in the parking lot where you had your last hug, that gut voice begging you to keep him home. Pendleton jacket wooly on your cheek. Your ear on his thrumming, beating heart. The smell of him: Irish Spring and the outdoors.

"I'll see you late tonight," he said and kissed the top of your head as your gut squished with anxiety and baby and Don't Go.

"We need you," you said or that's what you think you said as you rubbed your belly as the sky bruised up as you knew he was going as your throat shrunk and squeezed away your words.

"You had a premonition?" the chaplain asked hours later in the cool of your living room when he told you what your heart knew when you spied him through the peep hole: your husband was dead. Your bare feet with chipped red nail polish all ice. You just wanted socks.

You spun your wedding ring and wished the chaplain with milky grey eyes would Go Away.

You grieved. Hard. Cried beyond your beyond. You sobbed thunder tears on the stairs, unsure if you'd been going up or down when you melted on the burnt orange shag. You screamed at the unfairness. Your husband too young. Thirty-six. Almost a dad. You screamed until you realized Maybe Not. Maybe that's all the life he got and maybe it was right. Maybe there was more for you.

Three months widowed and your son was born. Six pounds nine ounces of yum. Your beaten heart beat, beat with love and possibility. In time love turned to more love. You remarried and had a second child. A girl this time.

"One of each," your friends said. "Lucky you."

And you grinned because, yes, you felt lucky again.

"It's going to hit us!" you screamed, glinting at sharp summer sun low in the horizon as the silver car blazed towards you as it crushed the rust orange Honda Element just behind the driver's door, that gritty metal on metal clash of bad dreams and frozen breath and Oh Fuck. You flopped around, squeezed by the seatbelt that would bruise your neck and chest. Ribs slammed into the armrest. Shins pounded the glove box. The Honda rolled on its side, this big pumpkin cut loose, skidded down the street, passenger window busted out, your shoulder inches from concrete, glass shards nicking your head, bare arms and legs, glass in your bra.

You gripped air.

Everything.

Slowed.

Frozen lungs. Your body went ice. Like dunking in a river past your eyebrows.

I'm going to die, zipped through you as you went numb. Body ditched, you became rice paper woman, floating out of the car and above the crash. No harp strums, no ohms, no Gregorian chants. Not even the sound of breath wind and yet. Yet. A tear in reality's curtain. You slipped through and witnessed.

Someone else's body pummeled whose hard working heart might stop.

She might have said I love you for the last time.

Then.

You were I'm Okay and This Is It and It's Good.

In that quiet sliver of Outside of Yourself you knew for the first time, knew in the tiniest atoms of your heart that when your first husband died, he must have felt this Unfisting. Bliss. Nothingness on the other side of sound. Nothingness on the other side of bodies.

And that's what made you cry.

After 25 years it took your own car accident to let go of your terror of your first husband being hurt. For 25 years you hoarded fear deep in your gut, past skin and muscle and bone, under your breast, a beat to the right of your heart. His crushed head, stopped heart, last breath, last words you made up to have some peace.

You floated above the Honda mess and knew: When he crashed, his essence eyed his mangled car and cooling off heart and said, "I'm out. Let's go." Because that thing we are never dies. Energy transforms. Your physicist husband told you that on those long car drives. Like he was preparing you for the unpreparable.

The rust orange Honda Element raked down the tar street on its side, wheels spinning.

Kids are too young, you thought. *Me too. Too Young.*

And swoosh you zipped back in your body. Reentry was faster. Harder. Waves of tingle rippled through your crown to your toes. An electric pulse in veins and arteries and corpuscles, in cells and mitochondria and atoms. Electricity radiated to your skin, arms, legs, toes, fingers, head. A wave up your spine, zapping vertebrae, vertebrae, vertebrae. Out your crown.

The door arm dug in your ribs. Your shins cracked against the glove box. You forced breath back in your fist-sized lungs. Forced. Like the time you almost drowned and your aunt pushed breath and life back into your wet six-year-old body.

For months particles of you hung out on that corner by Stark's Vacuum. You felt her when you crept through the crash intersection, almost reaching the speed limit, watching for the light change and cars streaming from the left. You didn't breathe as your body cooled with memory. You stared at Stardust You. Leaning on a street sign. Sunbeam crystals glinting off your coyote brown hair.

"What makes those little crystals?" you asked, pointing to an agate in the glass case, caramel colored, dotted with what looked like spliced crystals. Another, milky moss colored, with crystals like undressed winter trees, boney fingers stretching.

"Not crystals," he grunted, soft and low.

You waited a beat for more.

He wiped the glass where you'd set your coffee in a paper cup. The thin elbows of his jade colored corduroy shirt sagged.

Beauty and wonder all around you and your husband in the rock shop packed with rocks, crystals, salt rocks lit like beacons, fossils, a white cathedral crystal in the window large as a Dachshund. Cases of Montana agates.

Your husband wanted a bolo tie. His want drew you in. Equaled only by your want to please him.

"What are they?" you asked.

"Dendrites," he said, his voice tired.

Dendrites. From the Greek Dendron, or tree. In nerve cells, a branched extension where impulses are transmitted to the cell body. In agates, crystal-seeming branches, like ink drawings of naked trees sketched in the agate's skin. Growth but not growth. The illusion of time stopped. An illusion you can hold, loop with leather and wear.

You eyed a tortoise colored bolo with a burst of white, almost human shaped. "Ooh," you said and smiled at your love husband who laced his fingers through yours. Him. Deep blue eyes. Dove grey hair. Honey of a man. You could already see the tie at the base of his throat.

"Can we see that bolo?" you asked the man with the ponytail and chapped hands. "And the pendant next to it?"

You didn't know when you stepped in the rock shop, out of the Montana blue sky, so blue it was like being on the inside of a marble. Didn't know when the rock polisher swabbed his glasses and trudged to the glass case. You didn't know the healing qualities of Montana agates: balance, cleansing, window to the cosmos while held by earth. It's good you didn't know these things or you would have gone looking for your agate rather than letting it look for you.

You stood under the stars. Midnight black sky, speckled with pinpricks of light as if it were a worn blanket dotted with moth holes. The Big Dipper skimmed the treetops of Montana's fall horizon, scooping endless sky. Big Dipper. Little Dipper. Star shapes you've pointed to since you remember pointing. The cool of the stars. The cool of metal on your skin: your milky Montana agate with bark colored dendrites above your heart muscle.

You breathed the night in through fat lungs, soft hips.

You breathed stars, their atoms in you, yours in them. Breathed them into your body, your skin, the dendrites in your nerve cells. You on the edge of sky and earth.

Light tickled your fingers like when you were a girl.

The crackle of a campfire. Orange red firelight reflected in your dark eyes. The smoky scent lingered in your hair all night. The wind shifted and you smelled something fermented. Decay. Sharp and tangy and sweet.

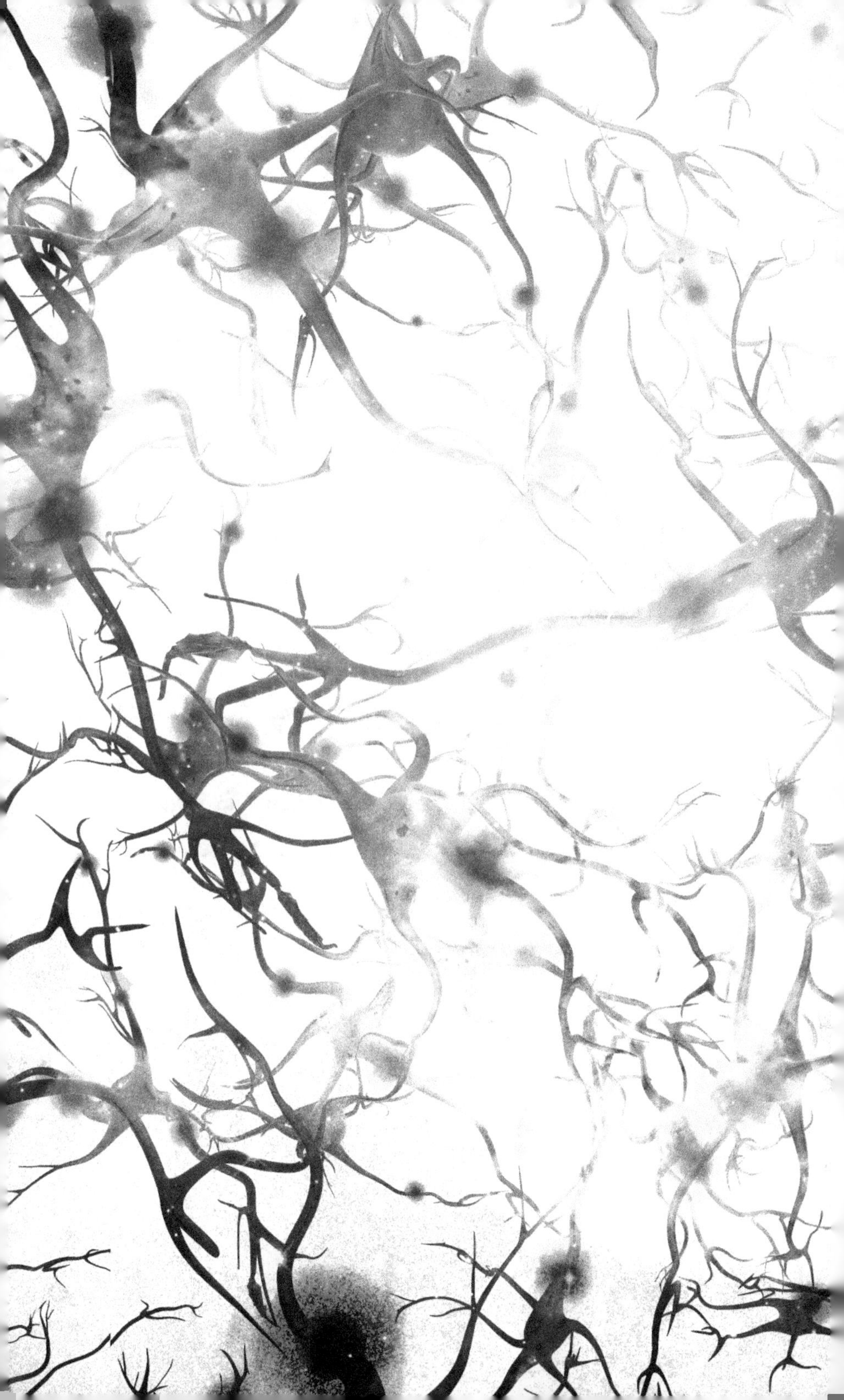

Writing Advice, NMW 2018

People often tell me they want to write. Me?

I say, then write. The way writing happens is by writing, plunking down in your chair and getting words on the page.

Yes, get inspired by being a hungry student: read, take workshops, find a writing group. Write. Write more. And know that your story is your story. Yours to write. Yours to tell. No one can write it like you can.

Anne Gudger

NEW MILLENNIUM

AWARD FOR NONFICTION

"Dendrites"

Anne Gudger is an Oregon/Montana/Oregon writer. Sea and sky float in her cells. Previous works can be found at *Real Simple Magazine, The Rumpus, Slippery Elm, Hippocampus,* and more.

She lives with her sweet husband. They have two amazing grown kids and a fabulous bonus son-in-law.

annegudger.com

HIDDEN IN A SUITCASE

Michele Leavitt

THE TRAIL WINDS AROUND THE BACK of Quaker Hill in rural Maine. It takes less than an hour to get to the summit, but I pack a bottle of water and some grapes and my notebook. This time I also pack my nephew's letter.

The tradition of letter-writing survives in families like mine, whose loved ones are spread out over the country in county jails, state prisons, and federal penitentiaries. In prisons, smartphones are contraband, so stamps are still currency. My nephew, Jesse Ray, is in a county jail awaiting trial. He can be held indefinitely without bail because he was on parole from a state prison sentence at the time of his latest arrest. He's 25 years old, and he's written me dozens of letters over the last seven years. I always write back, eventually.

The forest is still damp from last week's monumental thunderstorms, and a new generation of mosquitos has hatched. Far off the coast, Hurricane Cristobal pinwheels north and then east. It never makes landfall, but its outlier winds cascade through the forest's branches and down into the hollows, keeping the mosquitos mostly at bay. When I get to the top of the hill, the forest gives way to open fields marked off by lines of hardwood trees. Here, the wind is loud enough to silence everything.

From the summit, I can see hay fields and forests, a church spire poking out of trees, and more green hills. I pull my nephew's handwritten letter out of my backpack. Blue ink on narrow-ruled white paper. His penmanship is neat and legible.

> Dear Aunt Michele,
>
> Well here I am yet again. I suppose that adds me to Georgia's 87% recidivism rate.
>
> Not blaming anyone but myself for why I am back here.

At the end, he has signed himself "Jesse Ray," although I know he dropped the Jesse part when he was in high school. The compound name was too Southern, like Billy Bob, and his mother had moved him to rural Idaho when he was eight to get him away from our family in Savannah.

It's been more than 20 years since the day I met him at the Savannah train station.

To take my mind off the anxiety I felt at the prospect of meeting my family for the first time, I'd spent the 22-hour train ride from Boston to Savannah reviewing case files from my law practice. Born in the South, but adopted into a family from the North as an infant, I spent my childhood feeling as if I were wearing a flour sack while everyone around me was wearing silk, except when it came to reading. My adoptive father was fond of calling me an "enigma," a word I had to look up the first time he said it, when I was a 12-year-old drug user toting around a worn copy of Dostoevsky's *The Idiot*. The 19th-century novels a librarian had recommended to me did as much for my sense of well-being as the Librium my pediatrician prescribed when I rebelled against my parents, or the codeine-heavy cough syrup I started drinking directly from the bottle at age nine.

By the time I was 34, I had owned a successful law practice for ten years, which gave me the freedom to take time off when I felt like it, but that success came only after I had dropped out of high school as a teenager and run away from home, in favor of a life on the streets. After ten months of living rough, I returned to my adoptive parents' home, took up where I'd left off in high school, and then moved on to college and law school. I kept on reading and getting high on everything from weed to heroin because I enjoyed it—but I was able to abstain when I needed to complete an assignment or attend a job interview. Instead of being ruled by the brain disease of true addiction, I was born lucky, resistant. Importantly, I had become what is known as a chippy: an occasional user. By the time I passed the bar exam and opened my practice, I had a wide circle of acquaintances from almost every walk of life. My drug use tapered off during my twenties, but I never lost my easy rapport with people living on the fringes of society, and that helped me build a criminal defense practice.

I was exhausted by the time the train pulled into the Savannah station. From my seat in the last car, the platform looked deserted. Terrified that my family had decided I wasn't worth meeting, I slung my pack onto my shoulders as the train conductor lowered the stairs into place with a clang. I had deliberately dressed down in a hooded sweatshirt, sweat pants, and sneakers, in part to avoid looking like a snob.

A group of slim, edgy-looking people, clad in denim and leather, stood close together at the end of the platform. I recognized the members of my family from the photos they sent. A cigarette spiked up between the petite fingers of my sister Grace's hand, shoulders weighed down by the fringe on her suede jacket. My brother Tom was taller than the rest. Dark-haired and dark-skinned like me and our mother, he gripped the hand of a squirming towhead boy who looked like he was trying to jump off the platform. His wife Ida tried to grab the little boy's other hand. My brother Christopher's leather jacket flared out as he turned and saw me, as I ran toward them, as they spread their arms wide, and just like that, I was enveloped:

"Just like Momma."

"Momma's hair."

"Look at her hands."

"Momma's hands."

"Momma's eyes."

Talking all at once, hands grabbing my hands.

"She's crying."

I wept like I'd been cut open. I pressed my palms against their cheekbones, and my cheekbones into their shoulders.

If only I could have climbed inside their skin. My mother had only been dead for a year; she had suffocated from an asthma attack on the way to a hospital. So my brothers and sisters were as close as I'd ever get to my mother, who was 15 when she gave birth to me and then, almost immediately, gave me up for adoption.

"I'm too late," I wailed, clasping my sister's hand.

"None of us are too late. With five brothers, I always wanted a sister," she said tenderly. "You're still crying." Her own eyes were wet but clear, welling up but under control as we climbed into the front seat of a hulking Chrysler sedan. "Momma would be so happy," she emphasized.

I'd only known about these precious people for two weeks, since Sarah Muller, the private investigator I'd hired, called and gave me the bad news about my mother, and then the good news that I had siblings, along with Tom's address. An adoptee rights activist, she wouldn't tell me how she gained access to my original birth certificate and learned my mother's name. I'm certain that she bribed someone who worked in the hospital where I was born or in the Florida Vital Statistics office. Once she connected me with a blood relative, her work was done. I never heard from her again. She was a discreet person because she had to be; she operated outside of the law all over the United States, and was ultimately prosecuted on conspiracy charges for doing exactly what she had done for me: digging up sealed records. She served four months in a federal prison.

Tom called me as soon as he received my letter. A few months after I was born, our mother Tammy turned 16 and married a family friend, Ray. She and Ray proceeded to have six more children, and they stayed married until the day she died. When I met Ray some time later, he told me he knew she had given up a baby, but she had never told him who my father was, and the two of them had never mentioned me to the other children. Tom was surprised but delighted to find he had a long-lost sister. In the photos I sent with my letter, I looked so much like our mother that he felt like he was getting her back. The news about me spread through our family, and for the next two weeks I spent every spare moment either on the phone with a new relative or writing letters, feeling pulled toward Savannah, where most of them lived.

After we left the train station, Tom drove with meticulous precision through some of Savannah's squares, which are built around parks where old oaks drip Spanish moss and azaleas bloom in the shade. I wanted to stop crying, so they could see how happy I was. Instead, I started coughing. The car went quiet. My brothers and my sister knew from our conversations that I had inherited Momma's asthma.

"You gonna make it?" Tom asked when my coughing fit subsided.

"Sure." I flashed him a big, teary grin. I turned to Grace. "I'm fine." I didn't want them to worry about me, so I looked for something else to talk about.

I had noticed that the ignition had been popped, and a screwdriver, sticking out of the steering column, served as the car key.

"What happened there?" For ten years, I'd contracted with the state as a public defender just north of Boston, near where I was raised. Between that, and my own experience of living on the street, I knew full well why people pop ignitions.

Tom chuckled. "Lost the key," he said with a wink as we left the downtown area, taking the curve at the entrance to the

Broadhurst Cemetery and entering a neighborhood of tiny, single-family homes. Grace, her husband, and their three kids lived in a three-room bungalow on Temple Avenue—a bad neighborhood, she said, ruined by drugs and gang violence. Tom pulled the Chrysler halfway up her steep driveway, and parked it under a massive live oak.

To my astonishment, children poured out of the front door and mobbed me like butterflies on a New England milkweed field in summer. I wanted to wring out every drop of sweetness I possessed for them. The small ones threw their arms around my hips; the older ones patted my hair and pulled on my hands, and I heard the tune again, in a slightly different key, "Just like Grandma! Just like Grandma!"

I pulled my camera out of my backpack and started snapping photos. Grace's husband posed me with my brothers and sister and the children in front of a mass of azaleas blooming fuchsia, pink, and white. We swarmed into the house, and I began bawling again. Christopher hugged me. "You smell like weed," I said. He seemed surprised that I, a lawyer, would know what weed smelled like, but he didn't know much about me yet.

There was a loud bang outside. Everyone swarmed back into the yard. Tom's Chrysler sat in the middle of the road. The back end of it had knocked out a corner of the cinderblock wall surrounding the across-the-street neighbor's yard. In the driver's seat, two three-year-olds pushed each other back and forth. It was Jesse Ray and one of the little girls, Bee-Bee. They were struggling over the screwdriver in the ignition. The Chrysler's engine revved and stalled and sputtered out.

"Bee-Bee!" someone yelled. The two drivers stopped pushing each other. Bee-Bee launched herself out of the passenger's side window, flipped onto the asphalt, and ran up the driveway.

"It was Jesse Ray's idea!" she yelled.

"Was not!" He was right behind her.

"Boy," said Tom, "what were you thinking?"

"We was just goin' for a ride."

Spankings ensued. The men pushed the car away from the wall. Someone picked up the cinderblocks and wedged them back into their places, but it was easy to see that the wall had been broken. After a few false starts, the engine revved up. This time, Tom parked at the curb.

Later that afternoon, I drove with Tom and Ida to their home in Sardis, twenty-five miles west of Savannah. Their trailer sat on a wooded lot, shaded by sweet gum trees and jacked up on towers of cinderblocks at the corners. Once inside, my feet kept curling up and away from a nagging feeling that the suspended floor was about to collapse.

Framed, professional photographs lined the paneling in the living room. Tom and Ida's wedding picture—him in a shirt and tie, her in a flowery blue print dress. Jesse Ray as an infant, then as a baby able to sit up, then as a toddler. Jesse Ray with Tom and Ida. Everything in the trailer looked used to within an inch of its life, except for those photos, which gleamed from the walls. I turned around to see another picture, Jesse Ray with two older people: my mother and her husband.

It remains the largest, clearest image I have seen of her. She is smiling at the camera, but her eyes, my eyes, seem out of focus. Her hair is dark and flyaway, and her tanned skin is almost as dark as the circles underneath her eyes. Her cheeks are puffy in the way people's cheeks get when they are on steroids for a long time. There's an intubation scar on her throat. Her slender, tapered fingers, my fingers, rest on Jesse Ray's little arm. Her husband stands behind them with his hand on her shoulder in a protective gesture. He is 15 years older than her, but he looks vigorous and proud.

Tom cupped his hands on my shoulders in a similar gesture. "Momma loved babies," he said. "She loved Jesse Ray."

"And she was always pretty good around him," Ida said. "But you did have to watch her."

"Yep," said Tom. "Grace stopped letting Momma around her kids years ago."

"I don't think that was right, even if she did drink," Ida said. "She was their grandmother, after all."

"She could be mean as a snake when she was drunk," Tom said. "Most of the time she was real meek. But then sometimes you'd walk by her and she'd wrap her fingers in your hair and yank so hard your hair came out."

"She must've done something like that to one of Grace's kids," Ida said. "We never did find out what straw it was that broke that camel's back."

I lay awake that night in Tom and Ida's bed, putting the pieces together. Some of what I learned about my family came from questions they've asked me, like "You have nerve spells?" or "You like wine?" No, I'd tell them, I'm very calm. Wine's okay, but I don't drink much anymore because it makes me wheezy. I'd ask them about my mother's drinking. They told me she was a binge-drinker; she'd get some money and then she'd get drunk. Her husband didn't like it, and if he found the wine she'd hidden from him, he would pour it down the sink. He moved the family around often: from Savannah to North Florida, back to Savannah, then back to North Florida.

He'd been in the Marines in World War II. He was strict. He was handsome. He was a very good dancer. My mother loved to dance. Sometimes they took my sister and my brothers out with them at night, and the children watched them dance together like movie stars.

It was exciting to see the similarities between my siblings and me pile up. My sister, one of my brothers, and I all write poetry. Our mother loved to read. Some of us have "good skin," meaning we tan very easily and deeply. The Native American came out in us, and the story was that we had a female ancestor from the Cherokee tribe. Others are fair-skinned and platinum blonde, what's called "white-headed" in the South.

But I especially loved spending time with Jesse Ray, in part because his personality reminded me of the stories I heard about myself at his age. At four, he could already read, even though he hadn't been to school yet. He liked to draw. Everyone called him "artistic" in an admiring way.

That night, laying in a strange bed with strange pillows and unfamiliar dust made me wheezy. I got up and tried some yoga postures to relax my lungs. Triangle pose. Eagle pose. I used my inhaler. I got back into bed, but instead of laying down, I sat cross-legged, pulled the pillow perpendicular to my legs, and then folded over on it.

I've been doing this since I was Jesse Ray's age. It opens up the back of my ribcage and makes it easier to breathe. I call it my frog pose.

"Go give your Aunt Michele some sugar!" Ida said to Jesse Ray the next morning. I was standing next to the sink, drinking the cup of instant coffee Ida made for me. I put the cup on the counter and squatted onto my heels so that Jesse

Ray and I were the same height. He had gotten a cabinet open and was reaching inside it.

"Don't you do it, Jesse Ray!" Ida yelled, then turned to me. "Lord, he loves to take those pots and pans out while we're sleeping and start banging on them. Anything for attention." She turned back to her boy. "Go give your Aunt Michele some sugar, now."

He swaggered the few steps toward me like a sheriff making an entrance into a saloon.

"Who loves you, little man?" I asked.

He tucked his chin into his chest. "I dunno."

"I do!" I swooped him into my arms and kissed his chubby little cheeks a dozen times. Back then, I was 34 years old and childless. I'd never wanted the responsibilities that came with motherhood, but I did feel the occasional maternal urge. Now, I thought, I can have it both ways.

For the rest of my first week in Georgia, we played this game over and over again. *Who loves you, little man?* I had plenty of sugar to give him.

Over the next 20 years, I traveled to Savannah every summer. Some years, I rented a beach house on Tybee Island, and my whole family came to stay. By whole family, I mean those who were not incarcerated at the time, or so strung out that they were hiding even from their loved ones. Two of my five brothers spent most of their adult lives in state prisons for crimes committed in the service of their addictions. Crack cocaine twisted the minds of two other brothers, and their wives, so that they lost everything: their jobs, their homes, their health, their reason, and their children. And the children: Five of my nieces spent some part of their childhoods in foster care or group homes.

I had been happy to be a part of such a large family because there were so many people to love—and so many people to love me. But anger and disappointment and helplessness were part of the package. I realized early on that there would be many people to mourn. In the past ten years, four of my five brothers, and one of my nieces, have died from the effects of their addictions.

All of my life, I have been drawn to addicts. Maybe I admire their perpetual dissatisfaction, or maybe my affinity toward them is genetically hard-wired. Today, I am married to a man who is a college president, and who has been sober for 15 years. When I was a criminal defense attorney, I didn't just care about my clients—most of whom, as statistics would predict, were substance abusers—I loved many of them. It was often difficult for me to understand their self-destructive behavior. So I read the research and learned what I could. When I met my family, I had an added incentive to educate myself.

It didn't take long for my brother Tom's crack habit to become a full-fledged addiction. Ida divorced him and moved to Idaho with eight-year-old Jesse Ray, to get him as far away from my crazy family as possible.

Since then, my relationship with Jesse Ray has been sustained by telephone calls and letters, with the exception of two visits he made to Savannah when I happened to also be there. He was pre-adolescent at the time of both of those visits, still curious and active, but a little edgier. Once, he begged to have his almost-white hair dyed blue by a relative who ran a hair salon, and, after getting the okay from Ida, emerged from the salon with hair the color of a blue Popsicle. On another occasion, we made a life-sized alligator out of sand on the beach at Tybee Island. But most of his life from the ages of eight to eighteen was spent in rural Idaho, where he excelled in academics and on his high school football team. Like some of my brothers, he played guitar and sang. Every year, I received one of his school photos and a letter. I talked with him on the telephone occasionally, and when he got to high school, we talked about how he wanted to attend one of the state universities in Idaho. He called me for advice about going to college because I was his only relative who'd gotten a four-year degree. I gave him a few tips for taking the SAT. I was optimistic.

Over the telephone, I couldn't tell that he had already started drinking, but he had, and it wasn't of the social variety. He drank to get drunk. Just as he graduated from high school, Jesse Ray was arrested for breaking into a liquor store. Ida called to tell me. She didn't understand. She thought she had taken him away from the negative influences, but he was ending up just like my brothers all the same. She worked hard. He had a good life. He had so much potential.

The myth that addiction is a direct result of trauma is persistent in our culture, in spite of overwhelming medical evidence to the contrary. It would be reassuring to blame Jesse Ray's downfall on some external event. It would be reassuring if his fate were the result of bad judgment, or a bizarre childhood trauma, or the influence of bad company. Then we could more easily tell ourselves that it couldn't possibly happen to us, that our own futures and those of our children are predictable, and safe. But just as I will never know if I'm allergic to tigers unless I snuggle up to one, there's no way, yet, to tell if any of us are addicts until we start using. By then, it may be too late.

Ida moved back to Georgia while Jesse Ray was finishing up his sentence in Idaho for the liquor store break-in, and he joined her there when he was released. She hoped he'd learned his lesson. But in less than a year, he was arrested again; this time it involved a stolen property ring scheme and an impulsive, alcohol-fueled car theft. His cousins told me that Jesse Ray was off the chain as soon as he got back to Georgia, that this arrest was just a snapshot of months of drinking and drugging and doing whatever he had to do to get the money he needed to stay high. He ended up serving more than five years in the state prison system, where he read a lot of Nietzsche and Ayn Rand.

In the years of our prison correspondence, I never criticized his reading choices, even when I suspected they might encourage his tendency toward grandiose thinking, or his belief in the possibility of a super-man. I had enough faith in reading as exercise for the brain that I didn't question the content. Sometimes, I couldn't resist sending him books I believed were good for him, but mostly we just carried on a philosophical discussion about his changing views of the meaning of life. Sometimes, months went by without a word from him. I understood that these were the times when he was embroiled in the politics and economy of prison culture, or when the things he was forced to do to survive in a brutal community took up all of his energy. Eventually, he would write again and tell me he'd been out of touch because he'd been involved with the institutional drug trade, or with the Aryan Nation, or that there'd been some sort of lock-down. And soon I'd get a letter full of his thoughts about books.

> Just curious, have you read 'Guns, Germs, and Steel?'
>
> I had the opportunity to spend some time with it. Very good theories of cultural development. I enjoy that kind of literature because all of it helps me expand my universal viewpoint.
>
> I just finished Robert Greene's 'Mastery,' and he says it's good to study various unrelated subjects as that improves your ability to create and innovate.
>
> I was really looking forward to reading 'The New Jim Crow.' Unfortunately, right now my cellmates and I are in sort of a conundrum. The shakedown squad came and took our books. I didn't let them get to me. I am the embodiment of change.

An early frost fell this week in Maine, deep enough to kill off the more tender members of my garden: the edges of dahlias, the basil, and the hibiscus. The squash vines' leaves are shriveled to nothing, and all of their fruits are exposed. Some are still only the size of oranges; they needed more time to ripen. I wonder whether they will be any good to eat, since they didn't get a chance to mature.

I go back to the top of Quaker Hill with my backpack and another letter from Jesse Ray. It's the second letter he's written to me this month. I still need to write back to him, but what can I say that will make a difference? I feel as useless as I imagine Ida did the first time Jesse Ray was arrested.

From the top of this hill, the landscape is emerald except a few sugar maples with orange tinges around the edges of their leaves. I didn't see Jesse Ray this year on my trip down South in June, even though he was out of prison. Instead, I visited Grace and other family members who live relatively normal lives. I could tell from the extravagant tone of Jesse Ray's Facebook posts that he was getting high and living on the edge of another arrest, or worse. In my mid-fifties now, I'm too old to risk spending time near that edge, even for the chance to be loved. I'm too conscious of my own mortality and my own powerlessness to do anything but send my love out to him from a distance.

Regardless of the situation, there is always a small pleasure in being right—it turned out I was right about where Jesse Ray was headed in June. A week after my visit down South, he was arrested for selling methamphetamine and painkillers to an undercover agent. The headline in the local newspaper read, "Wanted Parolee Found Hiding in Suitcase." He must have been in some variation of frog pose. Like many people in our family, like me, his joints and limbs are very flexible. It's a genetic thing, like the asthma that killed my mother and that sometimes threatens to kill me, like the susceptibility to addiction that continues to torture so many of my family members.

From the boredom of a county jail where he is now awaiting trial, Jesse Ray writes about what happened when he got released from his last sentence, only a few months before this current arrest:

> For so long, 5 years and 9 months, I had been deprived of life's amenities, and I wanted them immediately.
>
> I began to sell drugs at first, then I used and sold drugs.
>
> Fast money spends fast. I managed not only to return to incarceration but also hurt everyone around me.

Twenty years ago, when I was a public defender, I heard that part of the story over and over again, and the beginning of it, too, which goes: "I thought it would be different this time." But it was never different. The man or woman who got out of prison wanted to celebrate, and that first glass they lifted in celebration, that first line they snorted, that first pipe to the lips set the story in motion again. There is no contentment, no such thing as enough.

"I know now that moderation is key," Jesse Ray writes, but there is no moderation for him, or for most of my family. There never will be.

I'm the only one of my mother's seven children who inherited her asthma. Like my sister Grace, and precious few other people in our family, I have a home, a job, and a life. Our one surviving brother lives most of the year on the outskirts of Savannah, in an outdoor collection of tents and tarps erected by homeless people, where drugs and alcohol are the center of life. Four of our nephews are in prison. Three of our nieces have had their children removed from their homes. Two others are in rehab.

So why them and not us? Grace and I both had our wild times, and we both made mistakes, such as running away from home, dropping out of high school, and using hard drugs. It's not that we grew up in more stable environments than other people in our family. For Grace, the drug use of her teenage years ended when she became pregnant with her first child, and she never looked back. Mine tapered off as I grew older and became more invested in my health and my career. There was no wrenching process of sobering up for either of us. Getting high was fun while it lasted, but Grace and I walked away from it without a second glance. Why? We simply didn't draw that genetic card. Either you're born an addict or you're not. For so many of the others in our family, it was never going to be that simple.

The hayfield at the top of this hill in Maine has been mowed, but the stubble left behind is still green, thanks to the summer's abundant rains. Sometimes, a mowed field stays green even under deep snow. I've seen it in a thaw: a memory of color seeping through a winter's dreary monochrome. I'm sitting on a granite boulder. Jesse Ray's letter is open on my lap, still creased from its time in the envelope, and I hold its edges tight against the wind. "I broke the law and I deserve to be punished," he says. I finally know what to say to him.

I take out my pen and write: "No, little man, you're wrong. You don't deserve that at all."

WRITING ADVICE, NMW 2018

Different people will find that different strategies work for them, so no writing advice can be one-size-fits-all.

However, a writer must write, and that means setting time aside to take that action. For some, it's early in the morning, for others, it's lunch hour, for still others, it's a week away on a retreat. Different strategies may work for you at different times in your life.

Other strategies that have worked for me are to pay attention to my surroundings, my past, my thoughts; to read widely and share my drafts with other writers in a small, supportive group; to let drafts rest for a while and then revise them, sometimes many, many times.

Michele Leavitt

New Millennium

Award for Nonfiction

"Hidden in a Suitcase"

Michele Leavitt, a high school dropout, hepatitis C survivor, and former trial attorney, writes poetry and nonfiction. Her essays appear most recently in *Guernica*, *Sycamore Review*, *Grist*, *Hippocampus*, and *Catapult*.

She's the author of the Kindle Singles memoir, *Walk Away*.

NMW POETRY SUITE 2018

Sarah Van Arsdale

UNDERTOW

The year my mother died,
hospital bed in her living room,
I flew to Puerto Rico with a lover
but even at the time I knew
it wouldn't last; she was afraid
of everything: the dark-skinned people
we met on the road
the volatility of Spanish.
She had never learned to swim
and stood on shore
while I dove into the thudding breakers,
then swam out to the sucking undertow,
pulling me farther than I'd wanted to go,
toward the coral reef
where seaweed tangled
around my legs and feet.

Not strong enough to fight the tide,
I swam, I rested, swam again,
tried to get back to the shore
and still was pulled away, not toward.
With just breath enough I lofted up,
arms flagging overhead, signaling to my lover
help, help, but she didn't understand
and thought I was waving in joy
at the sea, the sky, the sand.

Sometimes it comes back to me,
that terrifying tide,
the sickening roil of the waves,
how easy it would have been
to slip beneath the shimmer of the sea.
What a struggle it can be to die.
How difficult it is to love someone.
How easy to misread a cry for help.

Jacob Paul Patchen

DOG BARKING AT 4 A.M. ON A WEDNESDAY MORNING

What stirs us from these warm shallows
where daily thoughts and worries trickle
into visions of melting faces and debt-be-
gone solutions?

Intruder? Cat burglar? Here to steal away
the cat hair and still lingering smell of cat
piss left on this football armchair, from a
time when I couldn't tell Kirstin no?

No. This house is silent of cat burglars and
thieves out to meet their rapture. But Keela's
muffled, halfhearted calls into the night do
not fall upon deaf ears.

Does she know that I'm awake? Would my
dog child even care? Would she nuzzle my
tired hand if I were to stumble out into the
darkness and ask 'what's the matter?'

Perhaps she is having the same dreams as
me; free on the path that leads up through
the field where we walk for the view of
passing cars and ripe rolling hills. Free from
the debts of life, where slavery is an empty
dog dish and a sharp pile of unpaid bills.

Nicole Johnson

FIRST PRAYER

All summer we've set to tending
the casualties of my garden,
mostly hummingbirds, who crazed
with so much choice, smack
constantly at the playroom windows.

This morning your pudgy palm
pumps open and shut
around another broken, shimmer less thing–
A plea or an offering?

–to hold in your hands something
that just before twisted air
like a new quarter spinning–

That shocking iridescence draining
out before our eyes into the vague sheen
of a fly's wing.

I know what it's like to spend
a childhood brokering deals
with Saint Francis of Assisi.
To find what was swimming gold
shriveled up on the kitchen floor–
a dusty, orange rind.

Is it wrong to love how the sun
burnishes your bare shoulders
as you go gleaming from plant
to bowed plant?

To hang back and eavesdrop
as your shadow spreads across
the little makeshift plot:

bird *bird*

mouse

snail

bird

Rachel Berghash

DIALOGUE AND CHORUS

DIALOGUE

I want you to understand
that for centuries
I have been tilling this land.
I rise every morning
with the sun, its intangible beams
strong as my working hands.
I pray in a nearby mosque,
and dream of the Prophet
who rode a steed to the heavens
and beyond the heavens
above the Holy Mount.
I am bonded to this land
as a child to his mother's breast.
The walls of my house
are imbued with the spirit
of ancestors that embrace it
and guard it from those who
have invaded it time and again.

I want you to understand
my longing for this land
whose name has been vibrating
within me since biblical times,
a land I envisioned in dreams
and during prayers.
Everywhere in exile, pursued and
harassed, I lived in the shadows
of others, with the name of this land
murmured under my lips.
Mornings, I would wake to the knell
of sadness that seemed to be going
nowhere. But a vision of this land's
stones was a balm to my soul.
I imagined a patch of this land
to be a permanent shelter—
a refuge from a savage world—
I call home.

CHORUS

You yield to the shielding dark,
conjuring up a tree, a pond,
to calm what's left
of a contentious day.
You lie still. Nothing.
All is stale.
A host of confounding dreams
inches towards morning.
Upon awakening
life is a brazen foe,
hard as stone. Insoluble.
But the angel Gabriel alights gently,
turning the stone to tears.
All is tears that rise,
washing over you.
Why get up, you say.
You no longer seek grand gestures,
but blessed crumbs, a morsel of peace
to rescue you from oblivio

Ken Stahl

FOR JUDI

After midnight, after all
the sensible ones are in bed,
and the children tucked in,
you want to swim in the vast
Sea of Cortez. Such a woman!

Above, the stars overwhelm
the familiar constellations,
a map of chaos.
Below, phosphorescent plankton
stream water-fire outlines
of the motion of our bodies.
Constellations on your breasts, galaxies
in the raven-dark saltwater caressing your legs.

These bodies, alive
in the fertile moment
where the ocean loves the land
over and over again.

These bodies, weighed
with worthy excess,
those mussels in butter and wine,
clams steamed open over mesquite, oysters
bathed in their rough shell
in salt water, lime, salsa,
lifted to the lover's open mouth.

These bodies, worn
and worked and scarred, halfway
between the sun-washed beach
where the children ran
on bright shells of oysters, clams, mussels,
and the dark.

So, what is more amazing,
that the stars should come down

to dance in the sea
or that these bodies could still
look so beautiful to each other?

Harlan Bjornstad

PERENNIAL SELECTION

Residing now, as I do,
In the temporal mid-latitudes—
Some forty-seven degrees and leaning
Ineluctably toward a grayer North—
I find myself, in my reading,
More and more inclining
Toward the pleasures of return:
Toward attention to what previously
Had escaped me (the hero's briefcase
Set down at the platform's edge),
Toward affectionate annotation,
Toward that earnest daily conversation
With select authorial minds
That is the supreme privilege
Of the committed reader's reading life.

So away with the bright anthologies of youth!
Give me *Walden*, *Life of Johnson*,
Shakespeare's sonnets, *The Gospel of Luke*,
Then give them to me again.

Just outside my study window
The chickadees brave the neighborhood hawk
To alight at the feeder near the birch.
Black-and-white, flickering sociably
Through successive page-turns
As the sand in my hourglass sifts down,
They busy themselves in sorting
The sunflower seed that is their passion
From the remainder that is not.

If summer's fiercest flower invests
The full, studded disc of its life
In creatures so small, so deniable,
Surely these hours of study can nourish me,
Surely reading itself (the art)
Flourishes the more, the more
The light diminishes.

Cynthia Snow

RUBY-TOPAZ HUMMINGBIRD WITH PINKTOE TARANTULA

Why have you come?

Is it for color? My yellow
throat, red crown, purple wing?

Is it line? The still reach
of my beak, this grooved tongue?

Is it the rubbing together
of two unlike things?

I know you love
the small and the common.

Grub, dirt, fly, dung,
spider paralyzing its prey.

Did love bring you here?

Eggs in this nest will cool.

I will steal a last look
at a small triangle of blue.

The furry beast on my flank
will drink her fill, withdraw.

And you? You with the stone heart
and ready quill.

James R. Stack

APPLESAUCE

gradually
the trunk expands
as her family grows and spreads around the world
in time limbs are trimmed
when one or more passes in the night
the sour perfume evaporating with the expiration
her fruit born at a time of frost
worms carve notches in those found asunder
yet being plump produce the creamiest applesauce
aged and sweet to the tongue
she falls off the branch
escaping the maggots
leaving home and rolling downhill
in time turning nasty and foul and abandoned
with her seed loosely planted
after wintering over
a new breed begun under the snow and ice
tart to the taste
perfect for pies
wind whispering through the leaves
as they glance toward the other
feeling superior being on high
yet inferior to the sugar from the maple
there is always another
she knew this from the start
yet lived vibrantly by ripening fully
enticing the buzzers and fly-by-nights
like the widows in the windows on Mulberry Street
fanning themselves as they observe
the night creatures shopping during the day
bringing applesauce home
as a delectable side with the pork
bellies extended like the trunk
gradually

Ryan Hibbett

HAVING BOOKED A VASECTOMY

Give me an accidental third child named Townes.
He can sit next to me unbuckled in his flat-brim.

Together we'll peel away laughing from cheated
store clerks. Tilt Cokes at the noon Sun, piston-
ing their wholesome brown froth past our throats.

"Ma'am" we'll grunt at the scowling-circuit-judge
through sweat beads, knowing she kind of likes us,
or talk rain to newlyweds with stalled cars.

Sure the hounds will yelp. My pectorals will hang
like B-cups over the coiled engines. But I'll show him
where to clamp the sparking gator's teeth—black
to black, plus to plus—oldtimers stiff as cacti
working their toothpicks in the country heat.

At my hollar he'll hop into the driver's seat
and with a push of his bangs twist the ignition.

Oh Townes. Give me the thumbs up. Before I unhook
these cables and bounce into the whiskered mesas
I need to know you're not crouched in the truck-bed,
crying, it may be, for the lost strains of an ovulating wife.

Akesha Baron

HOME IS ABOUT THE LIGHT

home is where nothing needs adjusting.
i land softly.

if I slow down
i don't fall back into discontent, which is rushing.
place the spoon down gently; no banging around as if
anxious to be on to the next thing, the next place.

i hear birds singing in concatenations. i never heard
living sounds like golden rings, like smoke rings breaking and
then reuniting. Where else to hear, where else?

i am alive in a place i don't need anyone else to determine.
i don't need to be flashy. no more squirming. no more embarrassment.
i can handle such joy. feel without draining it off or letting it escape.
big enough for this joy of life unbounded, uncontained, unchecked.
no need to damp it down, cover it up, hide it away or pretend
it's somewhere else.

i no longer thought about anything, needed anything, assumed anything.
i did not need any weightless optimism.

then, in that openness, clouds parted,
heart came into being.

who knows anything about us
throws ash into stagnant water.
if you're awake nothing catches you.
you want nothing to do or say with
what happened yesterday.
you only want the light of home.

This work originally appeared in ***Snapdragon: A Journal of Art and Healing***, Winter 2015.

Bill Garten

PACKING

The champagne cork now a mushroom
Bottled in the heirloom blue mason jar

You unscrewing the lid tossing the cork
Towards the sofa, it lands on one candle

There now, you screw the lid back on
Place the jar in the box sealing it shut

When you were eight years old we bought
A praying mantis egg case for science class

Placed it on the window sill hot spring early
Summer sun cooking the two hundred or so

Babies looking like they would as adults
Emerged released into your grandfather's

Memorial garden of Hostas and lilies
His ashes of abuse now richer soil

The praying mantis egg case humus in color
Like the champagne cork

The sun giving birth like the candle he will light
Burning giving death to two hundred thousand

Or so memories you shared with him
Your fiancé drinking on the sofa thinking

What's left that was yours boxed up
Carried to my Chevy truck

You and me silently driving away towards
The moment tears hatch from the burn

Sarah Wetzel

MEDEA IN MIDDLE-AGE

It was an accident, she says to her husband.
Sometimes she says, *what else could I do?*

How many times, she thinks, I've cooked his favorite meal since.
They consider how the only reason they stay together

might be their shared grief, how infanticide can become the faded
first half of a metaphor, that the night is a dark mood

and desire take the form of a centaur with a beautiful speaking voice.
My love, he tells her, *nothing in Nature is supernatural.*

Though even this long after, he won't let her touch the remote.
On TV, a reporter diagrams the front line of a war.

Death connects us because so often it assumes
human form, an alchemy of fingernail cuttings and cheap

wine, crushed flowers and bile. Sometimes when he's angry, he reminds her
about the children. On Thursdays, they gather the laundry.

Time, she thinks, as she crochets him a sweater, is a lot like crochet
and how easily she mistook superstition for magic.

One purl, two purl, she chants, as she draws the blue yarn
back and again through itself.

Derek Mong

EXHAUSTED, RENEGADE ELEPHANT

Blunder of tonnage, passable trampling—

        the elephant, of course, is never   to blame.

Most catastrophes today, we'd almost all agree, involve handler malfeasance:

        whole systems asleep   at the proverbial wheel, the wheel

turned toward ease or profit.

        And so it seems with Tiny, tranquil now

at the squad cars' clumsy roadblock,   victim of a smoke-break swap in shifts

        (Barb in pachys, flirty; Bob in monkeys, horny)

that leaves a corn dog cart crushed.   Some folks fume, some blame the zoo,

        until the footage proves that Bob did all his jobs.

Which brings me to my child,

        blacked out in the back seat of our car, stricken with *something*—

moldy peaches? norovirus?—that'll cost him

        three of thirty pounds. We try to keep his fluids down,   but don't succeed

till the anti-emetics and IV.   Our doctor's face is a placid lake

        we stare into and sigh.

I don't suppose I have to share

        our fears of failed parental care   or the relief

when he returns to dancing on our couch.

The inexplicable scared us more than the sickness— the causeless calamity

that ate up a day. *Did you say day?*—my wife corrects.

Two weeks we lost learning how thin a thin kid can get—

and two hours Tiny spent uncaged. She crashed through brambles, rambled galumphing

until a smattering of sirens

caused her to pause. Here she is snoring like a semi in rain.

And we who've the impulse to acount for all carnage—

could we sing with the entropists who embrace chaos as pure?

We have, thank god, our tired metaphors:

the perfect storm, the act of god, and this elephant asleep on my son's floor,

a plush toy he carried from the hospital to bed.

He'll tug its ears, hug it hard then punch it in the head.

This work originally appeared in ***New England Review***, 2016.

Lisa Dordal

ELEVATOR RIDE WITH FAMOUS POET

After my sudden confession of love,
he extends his arm, patting the sleeve of my coat—

Is it raining? he asks—
like a hungry ant tapping on the abdomen

of the one carrying in its mandibles
a soft globe of dew

because doesn't the poet need the world
as much as the world needs

the poet? As a child, I watched my father
lean his body over our Chevy's

black complexity of metal. Watched him
draw out the looped end of the rod,

commanding an entire constellation of knowledge
in a single luminous pull—a language

I was never expected to master, only
to practice over that dense geography

the one small phrase taught
to my tourist body, my tourist mind.

It is raining. It has rained. It will have been
raining. And in the Coral Sea, just east of Australia,

the island that was thought to be,
drawn as it was onto maps, the new

following the old—this repetition of inclusion—
until no one believed it wasn't really there.

It wasn't really there at all. Even a whale
falling to the ocean floor

will be consumed, the tiny organisms feasting,
as if the water itself has teeth. Hungry ant

tapping on the abdomen
of the one carrying a soft globe of dew.

It is raining. It has rained. It will have been
raining.

This work originally appeared in ***Public Pool***, 2016.

Jen Karetnick

ELEGY FOR A GAMBLER

If it is true that "the dead have all the glory of the world,"[1] then so too do the missing, the lost, the stolen, the runaways, the mentally absent, the Krissy Houstons and Lamar Odoms found with lungs like water balloons, induced into comas with legal drugs, only one of them lucky enough to survive the race back into a society that will no longer offer garlands of roses because "we live… in feelings, not in figures on a dial."[2] Yet Amber and Silver alerts buzz our phones like low-flying planes with messages begging us to look, implore us to be witnesses, take note, as if in this particular age we are actually more aware of the world around us rather than less, only glancing up from gadgets to avoid walking through glass and into door jambs or knocking our foreheads against the woodpecker-splintered poles supporting these essential wires.

But the first time the unheard-of happens, no such warnings exist, so when the fifty flamingo chicks were snatched from Hialeah Park Race Track one July to be resold on the exotic pet market, "a very profitable thing to be involved in if you're a thief,"[3] no Rose or Rouge or Fuchsia alerts were delivered mobile to our inauthentic eyes and ears. No images of birds adorable with fuzz that stood out as if rubbed against rubber to create static electricity were sent for biometric identification. No *If you see this flamingo, please contact…* And perhaps there won't be a next time for this flock who, like so many citizens of this portmanteau city, *exilios* of Cuba, have planted their genetic code in such uncertain, urban earth, once considered by the natives a "pretty prairie,"[4] for generations now. When giving birth is the original gamble, keeping offspring from harm is merely a show parlay: whatever one gets, they all get. But the thief—he is the first gambler. And he can take many forms: Bird wrangler, horse track regular, poker player, brother.

My brother taught me to gamble with pennies on the floor of the den where cave crickets exercised their moon-landing legs the same year the Meadowlands Racetrack was born, the year of his Bar Mitzvah, the year he quit Judaism, the year my parents brought home the Siberian Husky pup he trained to attack and drag me down the stairs by my ankles as if hauling a live crow through snow drifts. Even though he cheated, always claiming the deal, labeling himself the house, I loved my brother enough back then to let him fleece me of my piggy-bank savings the way a farmer sticks his hand under a nesting hen for her eggs: I hardly squawked. Learning to play Blackjack, Texas Hold 'Em, Seven Card Stud—these were my own diversionary tactics. Of course they didn't work in the long term; a wager never does pay off that way. For those of us who give too much, there will always be recipients who want nothing in the end. The shared account, bloated by the drop and release of ridged, deliberate coins, waits. This time, when the alert sounds, it's in code, a terse range of monophonic blues that calls all our bets, and never again allows for a raise.

---

[1] From the poem "We live in deeds, not years; in thoughts, not breaths" by Philip James Bailey

[2] From the poem "We live in deeds, not years; in thoughts, not breaths" by Philip James Bailey

[3] Jorge Pino, the Florida Fish and Wildlife Conservation Commission

[4] Hialeah comes from the Muskogee words *haiyakpo* (prairie) and *hili* (pretty)

Georganne Harmon

AND CLAY

After Lucille Clifton, "Come Celebrate with Me"

It is a dream. A sorrow.
I've never run in the rain
to escape it, but run to meet it,
run for joy in its debate with sun.

I've never carried an umbrella:
I untouchable, unmeltable, unscorable;
so confident of being saved.

I never carried a painted sign
even though some were soaked
every rain that came, though some
ran every day from fear of loss,
from dread of pain, from floods
that drown. I've never stopped
on streets beyond my own
where babies cry I've never comforted.

Those lost and harmed
beyond my knowing:
I've never helped them make
some sense of what is possible,
and what is not. I've never lived
in tenements, I've never been
invisible while visible, except
my slow-poke soul. Maybe that.

Abstractions float easy.
The specific squirms in darkness.
A shovel. Love rises from dug-out
open-skin words that say,
that do. Only that.

Where is the bridge *between starshine and clay*
and how to find it early and walk it long and true
to the side of grit and shout? To I'll-come-too?
Rain can be more than joy and less.

Come celebrate every crossing
from the safe side of the stars
to where clay firms an instinct,
what kills, what saves, where I
will stay unsafe.

Jerico Lenk

HYLOPHOBIA

the trees do
not stop boys calling up mt. pelion for the teacher
of herakles, even as the boys crush spilled winter-
fire underfoot. the trees were here first and the trees
will be here, beech and arbor painted blue by cloud
cover, even when war screams fray into bracken
and thistle and little bones collapse like pine cones
in the path. they'll circle their haunted clearings
and dance their sabbat dance, limbs whispering
hymns, chimney-black bark choking back prayers
in the shape of tree rings. in their ancient, watchful
unspeaking, the trees do not stop the boys from
climbing to their highest branches and the trees do
not stop the boys' fathers from cutting them down.

Ryan Lawrence

MOST MEMORABLE INSULT

Flintstone is the man I see
whenever I meet a Fred,
the swath of five o'clock shadow
and blurred legs fueling a stone-cut coupe.

The furrowed face of the Duke,
eyepatched and tanned for *True Grit*,
has often scowled at me
for the droves of Johns
that I've shaken hands with.

What I'm getting at
is that you're more likely
to etch something in memory
if there's a strong image attached,
which I read somewhere long ago
and practiced like a monk since.

It's also probably why,
of all the times I've been dissed,
put down, trashed, and shat on,
there's only one smear that I remember,
only one slander that stuck.

It's when Gina said
You're nothing but a baby,
and I had just sipped coffee
from a hot paper cup,
I had just taken a hard drag off a smoke
and puffed out as the tip cooled.

I don't remember what wrung me up,
what made me bawl and rage
and be the swirling blades of a hurricane,
then later the placid eye.

But it's her addendum that cast
the insult in bronze,
a smoking, coffee-drinking baby,
and the scene it conjured,
that I'm helpless to erase:
little fat-cheeked me in a crib,
a nippled bottle dripping dark fluid,
tiny fingernails on chubby fingers
pinching a cig, so slender and white,

as I tremble in anger and start to wail,
but Mom leans in, cupping the light.

Berwyn Moore

FIG TREE

for Dolores

My friend, the scholar, is tucked
in a tidy room on Apple Wood Lane,

the name of her disinfected hallway.
She asks about the baby in my arms,

though all I hold is a book of poems.
She is courteous in her dementia,

uncomplaining as I wheel her around
the potted plants she greets by name—

Walter, Ed, Mary Lou, her eyes
squinting in the fluorescent light.

But the fig tree she remembers: *ficus*,
the sweet fruit she ate in her father's

garden. Perhaps that's where she
is now as she reaches toward

the tree, the puckered leaves
puddling in her lap, but no fruit.

It's *that old bald cheater,* Time,
she says, lucid, her laughter echoing

with Ben Jonson's wit before she
disappears in a haze. The *ficus*

in my living room has never offered
fruit, only shadows beneath flickering

leaves. Its thinning branches gauge
the changes here: my own survival

from state to state, from single
to hitched, from suburb to cramped flat.

I offer it a sigh, but I won't curse it.
Can it endure where I won't last?

Like my friend, I won't grieve time's
cheating. I will buy a stranger's figs,

perishable and whole. Together,
we'll hold the Adriatic weight

in our palms, bite the taut skin,
and swallow the immortal seeds.

Trish Lindsey Jaggers

THE DINGHY SPEAKS OF SINKING

They have no choice but hang on
to my sorry self. Effortlessly sinking.
The hole in me guarantees it.

There is no "flailing," no "struggling"
to what I'm doing, though people do
like to call it that. A slow leak and a fast leak
have the same ulterior goals:
take me down, let them down,
make me fail them. They say I take on
water, but really, water takes on me.
Broke, float poor.
The sinking ones struggle to keep me
afloat. They cup water and fling it—
handfuls of sunlit diamonds
return to the froth, return to me,
seeking reentrance. I have no say.

Water always seeks level.
I list, conform to its weight,
as it boards and boards and boards.
They still hang on. The rising harmony
of their cries—the sound
a clean window makes
as the towel finishes the task,
clears the water from its glass.
The surface now smooth, unbroken,
all breaths collectively held.

Laura Budofsky Wisniewski

IN FAVOR OF EMOTIONAL EATING

from *The Tears & Fears Café Cookbook*

An argument for eating to stifle anger:
You can shout all you want.
He'll never apologize.
He's dead.
An argument for eating to avoid sadness:
You can fall forever.
Bottomlessness is a real thing.
And also absolute darkness.
An argument for eating to fill abiding emptiness:
The stolen watch is shattered.
An argument for eating to dampen joy:
Isn't joy what led you astray?
Like a wolf disguised
as a firefly?
An argument for eating to assuage loneliness:
No. Nothing can assuage loneliness.

Desiree Hellegers

KODAK MOMENTS

I was four the year we went to Italy.
If I lay on the floor in the Sistine Chapel
—on my back like Michelangelo did—
I might have caught a glimpse of all those
angels. But what I remember is standing
in the basilica before St. Peter's feet, in awe
and eye level with his huge,
his perfectly sculpted big toe.
Yours was nothing like it, but we loved
to touch it anyway, a holy relic, a mystery
the way the cracked yellow pieces of it grew
into your skin, dug in and hung on for decades.
A baseball hit it when you were a boy,
and that bit of Americana nearly hobbled you.
I never understood why no one pulled out
the fragments the way they would have
shrapnel. Now I'm left to try to piece together
the history of your war years from that toe.

By the time the tanks rolled across
the border, you were already
schooled in stoicism. In a game of hide and seek,
someone shoved you—the youngest
of five boys—down the stairs.
You spent months immobilized,
a plaster cast of a baby.
When you were well and old enough,
you joined your brothers for their
weekly caning, beaten for something
you might have done, thought of,
or might do in the future.

In England during those war years
at that boarding school in the sheep
fields of Lancashire, you a Dutch boy
who barely knew English,
studied with the other boys how to
divide a rare, a precious egg
the way a jeweler splits a diamond,
how to take the sting of a ferula—
that strap of leather and bone—
without crying.
And what, after all, was a ferula
after the Blitz? After a bomb took off the top
of the hotel while you lay sleeping?
The way you told it, I pictured the stories—
coming cleanly off in layers, the way
a spatula might take off the top of a cake,
but never does—no blood or sirens, no
bodies blown into pieces.
I thought of cake.

It's more than thirty years now
since you died. I am two years older
now than you will ever be,
my body whole—the war took yours
in pieces—your teeth and heart
from malnutrition and pneumonia.
Now I think of that cracked toe,
what it might have meant in 1940—
the year you turned thirteen,
the German border only blocks away.

continued

You must have known the drill,
learned early what to do when
the tanks arrived, what to take,
where the jewelry was, where
the car was waiting. But what drill
could prepare you for mortars
exploding overhead, trees bursting
into flame, crowning in
a veil of smoke, your grandmother
in a ditch beside you.
What happened to her? All I know is you
arrived last at the pier, a child running,
then there was that moment when you
measured the angle, the height,
the distance between the dock and
the ferry beginning to edge its way
from the Hook of Holland to
the English Channel, that moment
when your family on the boat began
to yell, your father and mother,
your brothers, perfect strangers, shouting
directions, coaxing, gesturing, mouths gaping,
arms waving, open—all of them
coaches and catchers, all of them
leaning toward home.
You will jump, someone will
catch you, grab you by your belt—
your whole fragile, breakable life, and ours
hanging on that leather strap.

Laura Rand

WHEN A GIBBOUS MOON MUST DO

alone in the night
we envy
and the hurt is dark

and yes
our hearts
are endlessly broken

yet look—
the moon is compact
and winter-white

nearly round
nearly full
it holds just enough

I say this
because really
and honestly

who can stand on this nicked
and cast-off planet
that loses every day

and say
hey
I need something more

James K. Zimmerman

PAINTED LADIES

the day after you sighed
your last breath out
we let your butterflies go

your painted ladies

four of them born
from paper wombs
into a cheesecloth cage

now proudly decked out
in orange and white
trimmed in black

we let them go
with stiffened fingers

they would not leave

one drifted in hovering
half-hearted circles
another rested softly on your
daughter's wet shoulder
a third held close to the budding
milkweed you saved
from the scythe years ago

the last one content to stay
perched in its velvet cape
on my sunlit finger

we could not speak
so still
the afternoon

and when time began
once again to flow
they knew it was for them
(the opening of our hands)

another ragged breath was drawn
as they pumped and sputtered
(a single voice)
and took to the clouding sky

This work originally appeared in *Little Miracles* (Passager Books).

Sandy Longley

NOCTURNE, IN RED AND BLACK

Tonight, twilight
    I spot paw prints

on the roof of
    my neighbor's truck–

a fox, likely,
    out foraging for

mice, squirrels, sand crabs
    for three pups burrowed

under an abandoned
    porch, barking their

hopes and hungers
    a cappella under

April stars, dogwood
    scenting the air. Imagine

the vixen returning
    mouth full, her red-

gold coat lustrous, slick
    from rain, her forelegs

gloved in sleek black like
    the arms of one of Whistler's

society darlings during
    a night of dancing, children

awaiting her arrival home, eager
    too for tokens of maternal bounty

not unlike this fish head,
    this spine, this blood,

briny matter before sleep–
    a feeding fervent, feral.

This work originally appeared in ***Navigating the Waters***, 2016.

Cathleen Stewart

NOT ONE SPARROW

It is, isn't it, everywhere, everyday, the same:
I watched a seagull swallow a sparrow whole:
It was here, then, in an instant, gone.
I don't think it died immediately;

It went falling down the gullet
or descending or was squeezed along,
hard to name such an experience:
landing, arriving, splashing, resting
on remains of undigested fish,
flapping its wings barely, briefly, bravely,
in a darkness as sudden and final,
as in the beginning.

Anna Bernstein

FLY TRAP

When Casey's lover leaves her,
she finds a small paper
napkin crumpled
on the floor of her living room
is like a mild toxin
in the brain.
Or in the back.
Only a little rot. One good
thought of a plant, a succulent
owned by a friend, is enough to
drive it away, fend blight
up the veins and back
into the bean;
but there it is again, in the kernel
caught between tiles of
a sidewalk, or in the deep-colored hats
sold from out of dark
and musical dens walked by
on Fulton Street. No, it is in
her subway line—but not the car
at total rest, or at full speed
screaming past her on sacred missions
into the midnight tunnels. It is the subway
slowing down at her fingertips,
sliding past to open
the doors, yawning slack as a
lily in the morning,
breathing crowds out
against the damp cement;
it is a longing for a lily
that would not just as soon
close on her hand
as open for it.

Lisa St. John

THE WHENS OF NOW

When the gloaming begins and the sky becomes a Turner painting,

when the air smells of fallen leaves and cut grass and the dog is tired from her run and the cats are just waking in a crepuscular mood, and crickets serenade the last of the fireflies—that now.

When hero-bats flood the dwindling horizon light and frogs are in a brief conclave with the sleepy bees,

when trees turn silhouette from the bottom up and when the product of technology and nature lovemaking blinks on

one by one in solared garden lights—

when just before the darkening oranges take over for their 15 seconds of fame and we could be in the Sedona Red Rocks or in a field of Van Gogh's St Remy sunflowers,

when we sit on the rooftop in San Miguel de Allende drinking wine,

when, when, when this is now—if only for a moment. It was.

Oh, here comes the past tense again. Not yet.

Jim Glenn Thatcher

SPOOR

As I lay waking this morning
my mind slowly revealed to me
the two halves of my brain
as the dawn–clear print
of a cloven deer hoof,
or two bear paws, side by side.

These two images
appeared in palimpsest succession;
one forming quietly
    over the other
        without disturbance,
            each equal to each,

and as they came to be there,
I felt the stirring
of some deep and totem thing within–
the gathering of darkness and light
into a powerful and sinuous form
not yet known to me,
coiling and uncoiling
throughout my being.

My nature is trying
to tell me something:
Inside I see a new snow,
fallen for clear and joyous tracking.

This work originally appeared in ***The Cafe Review***, 1990,
and later in the poet's chapbook ***The Ur-Word***, 2008.

Roberta Senechal de la Roche

TIMEPIECE

We look for our place in things visible
grounded pillars, granite temples
flocks that return on time
blessing skies all over again
with the passing sound of wings,

Not the edge of storms
where everything might rise up
in liminal transparent waves
going fast enough to take you down
if you get too close.

Not the sea that also rolls its transience
over and over, spits spindrift
in our faces at high tide
as its terns and gulls go slide
to restless stony beds offshore.

But maybe you are inland, holding
your breath as you watch
her undo the final shoulder strap, deep
rooted trees in lulls outside, leaves
at their feet, snow settled on their upper limbs.

It is not that any of this exists
that matters, but how it might pass over us,
not minding annotations marked in red
or lists of names, of days, and laughter
or the color of her eyes as you move closer.

You do not want to hear the last word said
or see if she will turn or not
after you set the scene with a single candle
in the dark, knowing well what it might cost
to be invisible again.

Shay Alexi

RIPE OR PRO-LIFE OR THE DEFINITION OF LIVING

dedicated to Mike Pence

I met Life as a peach, a ripening violence–
a hairy thing matted heavy with sea salt a
tough skin, thin but screaming, teeming over, swarming–
a bee's nest.

I met Life as a bee's nest,
as a bee–
a honey-soaked threat, a violence sweet–
a violence mixed with earl grey tea, a self destructive thing that
in exchange for breaking skin all innocent
is driven to extinction
or worse than that–
the death of it isn't revenge at all, simply
indifference–

I met Life between the couch cushions of an antique shop, worn old pink stuff that
throbs, fabric with a heartbeat, corduroy, I met life
as a peach:
a sharp soft overflowing.
I look in the mirror and I meet a
sharp soft overflowing–
yet they are marching in the streets for the pits of me.

continued

they spit out my juices, would have me barter my fruits for unfamiliar stone things,
and my name
feels like pollution in their mouths–

I try to take inventory of them, like an antique shop,
but I cannot smell the history beneath their upholstery–
they forgot it,
shed it–
like my uterine lining
but not quite like that–
more polite;
they know not garage sale, antique shop, handwritten price tag, for they
are a furniture warehouse,
they have food poisoning in their veins–
fluent in languages I'll never understand, speaking in
rotting leftovers and stranger bodies
but those might be the same thing.

I tour each department of the furniture warehouse–
perfectly set hypothetical bedroom which I can never afford,
perfectly set hypothetical–
meaning the idea of a life–
meaning no one has made love in it–
meaning this is not home to bodily fluids–
not even tears–
not even happy ones–
you forgot all the juices
you forgot all the Life that you calloused your feet for in the first place.

there is a queen in these bones.
she is always home but she doesn't always come
to the door, she gets bored with trick or treaters–
not the little costumed purities,
but the giving and giving and giving away of sweetness–
it is bleached;
these open hands fried with dish soap lectures and french tips–
I met Life, and it goes like this:
I have dirt under my fingernails,
and cobwebs for hair, and you can tear apart my blueprint bones,
and I will
reassemble skeletons tempted to
dislocate your jaw so you know what it feels like to live in the space between
placed
and
displaced
but instead I will re-explain this cause you claim
I will say

I met Life–
as a peach
as a bees nest
in an antique shop,
and she looked a lot like me.

Megan Gieske

THE MAKURA-KAZARI

I know what keeps you up at night,
what crawled into our bed to sleep:
the fear that others are here,
that reincarnation is only the beginning,
and that sometimes you fear old ghosts.

And what would you do, and I,
if we could know for sure
that someone was there,
writing with fingertips
on the mirror in their hot breath,
"Don't grieve. Anything you lose
comes round in another form."

That someone, *her,* stood
at the head of our table,
saying that she'd been here
this whole time, that she'd been
waiting only for an invitation.
Would you invite her back then?
Even for one night, to that home
where you made love to me,
frantically and with desperation
as if to say *I still have you. You're still here.*

Aching to make this new. But it's not me
in bed, arching my back like a star
about to explode into tiny flashes
of pleasure, leaving my hot dense core
to cool.

In Buddhism, reincarnation takes place
decades after the death of a father, a dog.
But this is flawed.

In the sky, there is no distinction
between East and West.
After dark, bodies glisten like ice,
and the light between them
shapes something eternal. Not an angel,
exactly. More like a leopard
the way you bite my neck,
breaking it swiftly.

It was not an angel that carried me
upstairs that evening.

A holy host of lovers waited in a dark bedroom,
as the light slid through a cracked door.
Only the mirror recognized them.
This bed is never only ours.
And when they whisper, when you whisper
I bet you've never told anyone that before,
they'll remain faithful even if we don't.

That night, cleansing our hands
as if before a temple, we found
enlightenment just as I knew,
when I watched you undress
the first time, you were not him.

Have you ever wanted
to give someone all your lives?

Sarah Van Arsdale

TAKEN

The video of the girls
abducted from their dormitory
                    a spare concrete square
                    in dusty, far-off Nigeria
will begin in seven seconds.

While I wait, a white man on the screen
runs water from a hose
into a blue plastic pool.
It's the start of summer in America.
He makes a joke about his daughter—
how they can't communicate.
He's buying her a new cell phone.

In the video, the camera pans the girls
massed grey and black.
They are reciting words without apparent feeling.
There are so many of them, their shrouds so dark
that they blur into a single breathing animal.

My needs
are so easily satisfied
that sometimes I feel I'm disappearing.

I once was a girl, alone on a Greyhound bus
heading back to my boarding school
where no one was watching.
Classes were held in a reformed barn.
Smoking was allowed in the old milking room,
concrete-walled, stinking, freezing in winter.
We huddled there, child-refugees from the wrecks of our families,
and at night, found our way to one bed or another,
dragging our broken hearts.

I navigated the 1970s Port Authority
weaving among tight-skirted, beaten-looking women
and men who sized me up as if I were hanging in a butcher's window.
I was careful to keep my face expressionless as a penny.
Then boarded another bus,
which sailed out into Jersey
where I paced the farmhouse kitchen,
the upstairs rooms echoing.
Everyone else had gone: my mother to her new apartment,
my father to his new, still-secret, better family.
Only the house remained,
the stained glass window my father made,
my mother's fragrance lingering in her bedroom,
the books still on the shelves,
the willow tree weeping its branches to the wet, wet, grass.
Like a nuclear disaster
where the buildings are intact
but all the people are gone.

I could so easily have been taken.

But I wasn't, and now,
at last, someone is waiting for me,
wondering where I am and when I'll be home.

And the moon rose
a hammered silver disc
over the baobab tree.

This work originally appeared in ***The New Guard***, 2015.

Katharyn Machan

GINGERBREAD

1. Forest

Among crisp windows of pressed sugar,
licorice-button knobs, sweet drawers,
curving walls of honeyed ginger

she needed Gretel to make him grow,
that splendid boy with stone-filled pockets,
lingering fingers' crusty crumbs.

Obedient Gretel cooked golden-plump
roosters, curried dumplings, shaped
spicy cutlets into deep-fried hearts,

smeared thighs with currant jelly.
Stuffing, stew broth, soups, pate:
every possible piece of flesh

magicked to succulence at her touch
in that dark kitchen's perpetual heat
and Gretel dreaming of feathers—Oh!

and those bones she cunningly hid,
away from the stirring, away from the pot,
washed and patted beneath her apron,

safe from the Witch's spider gaze
and appetite for a male grown large,
made ready for her by his sister.

2. Hansel

I remember the Witch.
Skinny fingers, eyes peering into mine,
pale-bellied insects at dawn.
Oh, she was queen of all
my early hungers: sugar
milktongue, touch of silken honey,
every sweet my mouth could call for

and all with open door.
She knew I wanted more:
hidden jewels like cherry gumdrops,
pearls of purest white; against
those warm brown gingerbread walls,
what could I do but hunger?
The chicken bone, my silent tongue—

all play in time's sure cunning.
If not for Gretel's jealous hands,
I would have burned in her
dark oven, found the fire
evening brings: taste, taste
of stained-glass candy
answered prayers, desire's wings

3. Gretel

Why Hansel, Hansel, Hansel?
I wanted to eat, too,
gravies spiced with savory dill,
slices of beef with the fat still on,
rounds and curls and wands of pasta
warm and white with butter and cream.
Behind the shadowed cobweb cupboards

continued

I knew rainbow gumdrops gleamed
embedded in hard walls like jewels
I'd fingered in my father's dreams.
Dark chocolate stuffed with hazelnuts,
syruped squash so soft and dripping
it melted to gold on a spoon.
The witch kissed me three times

a day, making sure my mouth
was free of foods I carried steaming
to the boy in the small black cage.
No blood for me, no milk, no sausage!
Just a few leaves of rampion, wilted,
my apron strings grown long and longer,
my hands cold bone, my chin a knife,

my eyes a kitchen oven's deepest coals.

4. Witch

Eat
this house.
This honeycomb splendor,
these eaves
where gumdrop spiders spin.
I have boiled
dark caramel,
set rosy mints
just so.
On frosty panes
of sugarspun
you can write
your names
over and over and over
again in full moon's
syrup light.

Sweet children,
all my days
I mix and stir
the shapes of dreams
night steals from me
alone:
hot stars, perfect
licorice crescents,
cinnamon jewels aglow.
If I could swallow them
my eyes would turn
to toad gaze,
spring's free song.
Instead it's you
whose tongues must flicker
in and out with delight.

This fire spits.
My iron spoon
grows heavy,
sears my flesh.
Can you count
the candied cherries
lined up in a row?
Taste them now
and the crystal drops
I pretend are tears.
Grow fat.
Uncage your fears
of who I really am.
Just once call me
Pure Dark Mother
before the oven slams.

Nan Becker

VERITY

The river, under hoarfrost air, is ice-taut. Here and gone
are the color of ash. Large patient wings shadow possibilities
below—smaller heartbeats hidden underground who cannot

understand—their own breaths with the pure want to live,
would not save them. This will-less goings-on, recoil and relief,
press to continue as if pitched by their own volition though even

now, again, again, I see it all mostly comes by chance. Nothing
of the time between first breath and last, lasts—as if none of this
happened, as it always has, until light and dark are gone.

Ruth Thompson

HERO'S RETURN

When the hero comes back
from her journey

she is in the greatest danger of all.
The jaws of the ordinary

close around her ankles.
The tendrils of her other stories

fill her mouth. That shape
she left behind, empty,

slides up around her and snaps
to. She might never have gone.

Odysseus went away again,
then, to a place where no one

had ever heard of the sea
and there at last he died.

But Penelope, when she returns,
comes back to the loomwork

into which she has already
been woven. Unpicking

those threads is harder
than unmaking a shroud

at night. Nor can she say
if it is a shroud she needs

after all, here in Ithaca,
or a cleverer weaver.

Vernon Waring

CONCLUSION

someone still likes
the way words
race across a page
like brazen insects

someone still marvels
at the magic and movement
of poetry
rhythms that challenge
and calm the heart

someone still respects
the simple music
of a single sonnet
so sweetly sounding
the reader whirls
in exhilaration
like a ballerina
in a sunlit room

now take the words
and make them twist
and turn and jump
and rise and fall

you are their master
their leader their captain
make them bow to your voice
make them cower and despise you
call you hateful names
curse your power

bind them up
in a choke hold
watch the blood
fill their faces
their tiny mouths
squealing in pain

then release them slowly
into the night
whispering your forgiveness
currying their favor
for you know
in their fucking humility
in their confusion and fear
they are
after all
only words

CONTRIBUTORS

NOTES ON CONTRIBUTORS

Akesha Baron holds a PhD in sociocultural anthropology. Her poems have been finalists for the Patricia Dobler Poetry award, the Atlanta Review Poetry competition, and appear in *Snapdragon, ESME* and *Washington 129*. She is an ordained novice Zen priest and an analyst in training at the C.G. Jung Institute of New York.

Nan Becker's book of poems is *After Rain* (Elephant Tree House, 2011 elaphanttreehouse.com). Poems are forthcoming or have appeared in *The Common Ground Review, Cloudbank 2, The Meadow, Nimrod, New Millennium Writings, Redivder, Red Rock Review, Salamander* and elsewhere. She lives in Stillwater, NJ.

Rachel Berghash is a prolific poet and Pushcart Prize nominee. Her poetry and translations appear in numerous literary magazines. She holds a master's degree in social work from Yeshiva University and is a longtime teacher of Interior Life seminars that use key philosophical, psychological, and religious texts. Her essays in this area, with co-author Katherine Jillson, have been published in *Tikkun*, the *Journal of Religion and Health*, and elsewhere.

Anna Bernstein is a writer from Brooklyn, where she also works as a historical research assistant and copy editor. She has been published in *decomp magazine, Dunes Review, Reed Magazine, Carve Magazine*, and others. She enjoys writing about everything from Jewishness to disability to animal behavior to the occult.

Katie Bickham's book, *The Belle Mar* (2015), won the Lena-Miles Wever Todd Poetry Prize. Katie's poems have appeared in *Rattle, Southern Quarterly, Prairie Schooner, Pleiades, The Missouri Review*, and elsewhere. She received The Missouri Review Editor's Prize and an SLS fellowship. Katie teaches creative writing at Bossier Parish Community College.

Harlan Bjornstad lives in Valparaiso, Indiana, with his wife. He has written and produced three plays and is presently working on a novel about growing up in a missionary family in Kodaikanal, South India.

Cassady Black lives in Colorado, where she is a writer, editor, and consultant. She is a founding editor of *Slow Trains Literary Journal* (slowtrains.com), and her writing has been published in *Eclectica, Salon.com,* and *The Best American Erotica series*, among others. cassadyblack.com

Alexis Williams Carr has been a part of *NMW* since its founding in 1996, first as a humble envelope stuffer and errand runner, before working her way up to entry screener, then assistant editor. She graduated Magna Cum Laude from Middle Tennessee State University with a BA in English Literature. After working in higher education and in corporate communications and publishing, Alexis was thrilled to take over as Editor of *New Millennium Writings* in 2012. She has to date published hundreds of writers within the pages of *NMW* and looks forward to many more years of awarding and publishing new and emerging writers.

Lisa Dordal, author of *Mosaic of the Dark,* teaches at Vanderbilt University. A Pushcart Prize nominee and recipient of an Academy of American Poets Prize, her poetry has appeared in *Best New Poets, CALYX, The Greensboro Review, Vinyl Poetry,* and *Ninth Letter*. lisadordal.com

Bill Garten's *Asphalt Heart* was published by Main Street Rag Publishing 2018. Its chapbook version was a finalist in The Comstock Review's 2017 Jessie Bryce Niles Chapbook Contest. Bill was a Finalist in 2018 Tucson Festival Books' Literary Awards and winner of Antioch's Writers 2018 Workshop Judson Jerome Scholarship.

Megan Gieske is a wandering poet. From her home in New Jersey, she has traveled the world as an artist and advocate, telling stories that bring people closer together. Follow her poetry journey on Instagram @ MeganGieske and Facebook @MeganGieskeOfficial.

Anne Gudger is an Oregon/Montana/Oregon writer. Sea and sky float in her cells. Previous works can be found at *Real Simple Magazine, The Rumpus, Slippery Elm, Hippocampus,* and more. She lives with her sweet husband. They have two amazing grown kids and a fabulous bonus son-in-law. annegudger.com

Georganne Harmon grew up in Nashville, Tennessee, where she now makes her home. Her poems have appeared in various journals, and she has been the recipient of four New Millennium Writings awards as well as six Tennessee Writers Alliance awards and an award from Tennessee Mountain Writers. Her first chapbook bears the title ***We Will Have Ghosts***. She has recently completed a novel, *Labyrinth*, now in search of a publisher. Ms. Harmon has been a lifelong teacher and currently facilitates workshops for adult writers in Middle Tennessee.

Desiree Hellegers is an associate professor of English at Washington State University Vancouver and author of the oral history collection *No Room of Her Own: Women's Stories of Homelessness, Life, Death and Resistance* (Palgrave 2011). She lives in Portland, Oregon.

Ryan Hibbett is an Assistant Professor of Literature and Composition at Northern Illinois University.

Miah Jeffra is the author of *The First Church of What's Happening* (Nomadic Press, 2017). They have been awarded the Sidney Lanier Prize and Clark-Gross Award for fiction, and a 2014 Lambda Literary Fellowship for nonfiction. Miah is editor of the queer literary collaborative, Foglifter Press.

Trish Lindsey Jaggers' "Crazy-Eights" goal as a poet is to, "Create simply: Write so an eight-year-old can read it, an eighteen-year-old can understand it, and an eighty-year-old will have lived it." The author of *Holonym: poems* (FLP, 2016), Jaggers teaches English and creative writing at Western Kentucky University.

Nicole Johnson teaches creative and critical writing at the University of San Diego and Art Center/Pasadena.

Jen Karetnick was the winner of the 2018 Split Rock Review Chapbook Competition for *The Crossing Over* (May 2019), authored *The Treasures That Prevail* (Whitepoint Press, September 2016), finalist for the 2017 Poetry Society of Virginia Book Prize. Her work appears in *Ovenbird, Salamander,* and *Tampa Review*.

Ryan Lawrence is an award-winning writer living in Portland, Oregon. His awards include the 1991 Presidential Physical Fitness Award and an Honorable Mention for a science fair project about dinosaurs. His girlfriend, Bailey, adores him endlessly.

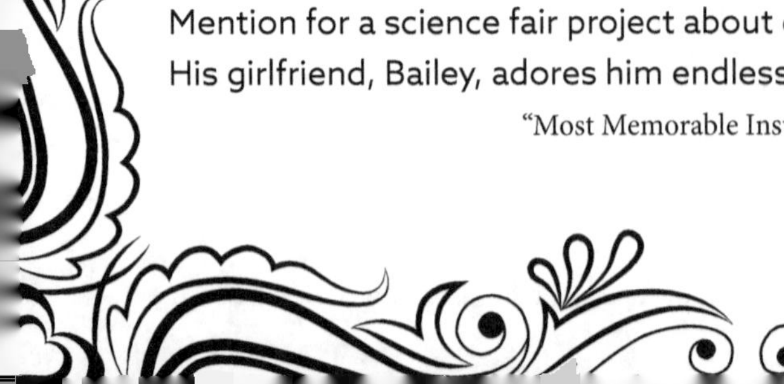

Michele Leavitt, a high school dropout, hepatitis C survivor, and former trial attorney, writes poetry and nonfiction. Her essays appear most recently in *Guernica, Sycamore Review, Grist, Hippocampus,* and *Catapult*. She's the author of the Kindle Singles memoir, *Walk Away*.

Jerico Lenk is a USF Tampa undergrad, Seattlite at heart, studying Creative Writing, Russian and Western European history, and Classics. jericolenk.com

Sandy Longley is an Associate Professor of English of English at Columbia-Greene Community College. Her collection of poems called *Navigating the Waters* was published in 2016 by Finishing Line Press.

Katharyn Howd Machan, author of 34 published collections (most recently *Dreaming Turquoise*, winner of the 2017 Red Berry Editions chapbook competition, and *Dark Matters* from FutureCycle Press) has had poems appear in numerous magazines, anthologies, and textbooks, including *The Bedford Introduction to Literature and Sound and Sense*. A resident of Ithaca, New York since 1975, she was Tompkins County's first poet laureate. She is a professor in Ithaca College's Writing Department and former director of the Feminist Women's Writing Workshops.

Mary Makofske's latest books are *World Enough, and Time* (Kelsay, 2017) and *Traction* (Ashland, 2011), winner of the Richard Snyder Prize. Her poems have appeared in *Poetry, Southern Poetry Review, Poetry East, Antiphon, Poetry Daily*, and in eighteen anthologies. She received the 2017 International Poetry Prize from Atlanta Review. marymakofske.com

Evan McMurry's fiction has been published in more than a dozen journals, including *Post Road, Euphony, Arcturus, Oddville Press, Palaver,* and more. His story "The Fall of Rabbi Gold" was selected as a finalist for the Al-Simāk Award for Fiction from the Chicago Review of Books.

Derek Mong is the author of two poetry collections—*Other Romes* (2011) and *The Identity Thief* (2018)—and a forthcoming chapbook of Latin adaptations. New work can be found in the *Kenyon Review, Pleiades*, and *Blackbird*. He is the Byron K. Trippet Assistant Professor of English at Wabash College.

Berwyn Moore's third book, *Sweet Herbaceous Miracle*, won the 2017 John Ciardi Prize from BkMk Press. Her poems have appeared in *Five Points Journal*, where she won the James Dickey Prize, *Measure: A Review of Formal Poetry, Nimrod, JAMA,* and other journals. She teaches at Gannon University in Erie, Pennsylvania.

Jacob Paul Patchen was born and raised outside of Byesville, Ohio where he spent his youth tormenting babysitters and hiding in trees. Patchen earns his inspiration through experience, where he writes abundantly about love, war, sex, family, and drinking. Jacob is a poet, a blogger, an author, and a combat veteran.

"Dog Barking at 4 a.m. on a Wednesday Morning" © 2016 Jacob Paul Patchen

Laura Rand lives in the foothills of the Sierra Nevada. She is a self-taught writer and naturalist, cyclist and TBI survivor. Her poems have appeared in *NMW (New Millennium Writings), Tiger's Eye, Manzanita, Poetry Now, Ship of Fools, Freefall,* and elsewhere. Her first collection of poetry, *to unfold a fist*, was published by Tiger's Eye Press, 2015.

"When a Gibbous Moon Must Do" © 2016 Laura Rand

Lisa St. John is a high school English Teacher and published poet. She lives in the beautiful Hudson Valley of upstate New York where she calls the Catskill Mountains home. Her first chapbook, *Ponderings*, can be purchased at Finishing Line Press. Lisa has published her poetry in the *Barbaric Yawp, Bear Creek Haiku, Misfit Magazine, The Poet's Billow PKA's Advocate, Haight Ashbury Literary Journal, The Ekphrastic Review,* and *Chronogram Magazine*. The poem "There Must Be a Science to This" won The Poet's Billow's Bermuda Triangle Contest and "Mowing the Lawn" was shortlisted for the Fish Poetry Prize and later published in *Fish Anthology 2016*. When she is not reading or writing longer pieces, Lisa enjoys thinking out loud on her blog, *Random Mind Movements*. lisastjohnblog.com

"The Whens of Now" © Lisa St. John

Roberta Senechal de la Roche teaches at Washington and Lee University and lives in the woods near Free Union, Virginia. Her poems have appeared in *Literary Juice, Still: The Journal, Front Porch Review, Colorado Review, Yemassee, Cold Mountain Review,* and elsewhere. She is finishing a volume of poems called *Going Fast*.

Adam Sifre is a fifty-something writer, hiding out in the wilds of North Jersey. He has three children, an imaginary dog, and many friends, and suspects none of them have read his work. He's the author of *I've Been Deader,* a near-perfect blend of horror and comedy.

Cindy Snow's writing has been nominated for a Pushcart, has appeared in the *Massachusetts Review, Peace Review,* and elsewhere, and in 2016, Slate Roof Press published her chapbook, *Small Ceremonies*. Her recent manuscript focuses on the 17th Century naturalist, Maria Sibylla Merian. Cindy works at Greenfield Community College, MA.

James R. Stack is a recipient of the Freedom of Expression of Courage Award from PEN America. He has self-published a collection of poetry, *PLEASURES & SEASONS OF VERMONT*. His poems have appeared in ENGLYN, *America Is Not the World* (Pankhearst Anthology), *Ash & Bones,* among others.

Ken Stahl is a poet from Tucson, Arizona.

Cathleen Stewart is an emerging poet, emerging out of retirement, though she has been writing poems since high school and has had several published. She has an M.F.A. (in Creative Writing) and an M.A. (in Philosophy). Her education and lifelong experience bring longitudinal richness to her poetry. Cathleen's central focus is the role history and language play in shaping our personal experience.

Shay Alexi is a poet, storyteller, and dog enthusiast based out of Atlanta, GA. Shay likes to write things that are somewhere between a magic trick, a pile of sweat, and a text from your best friend. (The world needs a little wonder, a little mess, and a lot of love.) You can find Shay's work in video form on *Button Poetry, Write About Now,* and *Homegrown Poetry*. Shay's piece, "I Used to Say I Hated My Hometown," was published in *Beecher's Literary Mag* as the winner of their 2017 poetry contest, and another piece, "Creases," was published in *RiversEdge Literary Journal*. Shay is a member of Atlanta's Java Monkey Slam Team and represented them in Denver at the 2017 National Poetry Slam.

Jim Glenn Thatcher has had twelve poems published in *New Millennium Writings* since 2011—two First Prizes and ten Honorable Mentions, two of them shortlisted for First. Jim grew up in books and the woods in the Adirondacks, a mental atmosphere still with him. His themes are Time and Nature, and he lives and writes them. He'll be sending more to *NMW*.

Ruth Thompson is the author of *Whale Fall & Black Sage* and three other books of poetry. Her "fierce, gorgeous, sensual" poems have won many national awards, been nominated for the Pushcart Prize, and been choreographed and performed collaboratively with dancers Shizuno Nasu and others.

Sarah Van Arsdale is the author of four books of fiction, including *Toward Amnesia* and *In Case of Emergency, Break Glass*. Her fifth book, *The Catamount*, a narrative poem with her illustrations, was published by Nomadic Press in May, 2017. She teaches in the Antioch/LA MFA program. sarahvanarsdale.com

Vernon Waring's poetry has appeared in *Ascent Aspirations Magazine, Nerve Cowboy, The Great American Poetry Show,* and *The Iconoclast*. His short fiction has been singled out for commendation in the *Glimmer Train, New Millennium Writing Awards,* and *Soul-Making Literary Competitions*. A native of Philadelphia, he now lives in King of Prussia, Pennsylvania.

Sarah Wetzel is the author of *River Electric with Light,* which won the 2013 AROHO Poetry Publication Prize and *Bathsheba Transatlantic,* which won the Philip Levine Prize for Poetry and was published in 2010. Sarah currently teaches creative writing at The American University of Rome.

Laura Budofsky Wisniewski's work has appeared in *Hunger Mountain Review, American Journal of Poetry, Saranac Review, Confrontation,* and others. She is a 2018 Pushcart nominee. Her chapbook, *How to Prepare Bear,* is forthcoming.

"In Favor of Emotional Eating" © Laura Budofsky Wisniewski

James K. Zimmerman is an award-winning poet and Pushcart Prize nominee. His work appears in *Pleiades, Chautauqua, The Evansville Review, Nimrod, Kestrel, The Cape Rock,* and *Confrontation,* among others. He is the author of *Little Miracles* (Passager, 2015) and *Family Cookout* (Comstock, 2016), winner of the Jessie Bryce Niles Chapbook Prize.

"Painted Ladies" © 2011 James K. Zimmerman

Image Credits:

Photo © Jelle Krings | Dreamstime.com | 11* | 114–115 *edited

Photo © Sylvie Pabion | Dreamstime.com | 12

Photo by Jeremy Bishop | 14

Photo by Josh Wilburne | 17

Photo by Lance Asper | 29

Photo by Alexis Fauvet | 37

Photo by Jason Wong | 40

Photo by Elijah O'Donnell | 55*

Photo by Denys Nevozhai | 77 | 78

Photo by Ryoji Iwat | 92

Photo by J W | 111*

Photo © Lukas Bischoff | Dreamstime.com | 79 | 184–185 | 194–195 | 198*–201

Photo by Bry Ulrick | 206–207

Photo by Angie Corbett-Kuiper | 196–197 | 215*

Photo by Sam Mathews | 214–215

Photo © Trungdbnguyen | Dreamstime.com | 210–211 | 216

Larry Harvey photographed with Polaroid 665 film by Tony Deifell | 190

BACK MATTERS

SUBMISSIONS

How to Submit Your Work

From single poems, short stories, and essays to book-length works, novellas, collections, and all experimental spaces in between, NMW + SUNSHOT PRESS + MUSEPAPER is where you want your words to be.

Visit us on the interwebs:

NEWMILLENNIUMWRITINGS.ORG

SUNSHOTS.ORG

Can't find what you're looking for? Email us:

HELLO@NEWMILLENNIUMWRITINGS.ORG

Colophon Key

Doldrums Near the End of Empire 13
Author: Azo Sans, Regular, 10 pt
Title: Azo Sans Uber, Regular, 16 pt | 19 ld
Body: LTC Caslon, Pro Regular, 10.5 pt | 12.5 ld

Shorn 18
Author: Azo Sans, Regular, 10 pt
Title: Azo Sans Uber, Regular, 16 pt | 19 ld
Body: Whitman, Roman, 11 pt | 13 ld

Papa's Parrot 23
Title: Azo Sans Uber, Regular, 26 pt | 31 ld
Author: Azo Sans, Bold, 16 pt
Body: Minion Pro, Regular, 12 pt | 15 ld

Growl 31
Title: Azo Sans Uber, Regular, 26 pt | 31 ld
Author: Azo Sans, Bold, 16 pt
Body: Minion Pro, Regular, 12 pt | 15 ld

Nothing Kinky 39
Title: Azo Sans Uber, Regular, 26 pt | 31 ld
Author: Azo Sans, Bold, 16 pt
Body: Californian FB, Regular, 12 pt | 15 ld

Mapping Hana 57
Title: Azo Sans Uber, Regular, 26 pt | 31 ld
Author: Azo Sans, Bold, 16 pt
Body: Adobe Garamond Pro, Regular, 12 pt | 15 ld

Dendrites 79

Title: Azo Sans Uber, Regular, 26 pt | 31 ld
Author: Azo Sans, Bold, 16 pt
Body: Adobe Caslon Pro, Regular, 12 pt | 15 ld

Hidden in a Suitcase 91

Title: Azo Sans Uber, Regular, 26 pt | 31 ld
Author: Azo Sans, Bold, 16 pt
Body: Ten Oldstyle, Regular, 12 pt | 15 ld

Poetry Suite 132+

Author: Azo Sans, Regular, 10 pt
Title: Azo Sans Uber, Regular, 16 pt | 19.5 ld
Body: Adobe Caslon Pro, Regular, 10 pt | 12 ld

A few notes:

Sizes are rounded to the nearest .5pt.

Body typefaces will likely include multiple fonts. (regular, italic, bold, etc.)

When Brent first became interested in book design, a big frustration was the surprising scarcity of resources to compare different typefaces in action.

If you found this at all useful, please do let Brent know, along with any suggestions you may have.

As long as *one person* finds this key beneficial we will continue to include it in future publications.

Email: colophon@newmillenniumwritings.com

LIVE

"We're not hiding from the world, we're trying to change it."

—Larry Harvey

1948—2018

ARTIST, ACTIVIST, CO-FOUNDER OF BURNING MAN

www.ingramcontent.com/pod-product-compliance
Lightning Source LLC
Chambersburg PA
CBHW070639170726
48291CB00003B/1063

* 9 7 8 1 9 4 4 9 7 7 2 7 6 *